"There!" Tiffany had cried.

"Sara!"

Would Tiffany ever forget the agony in Peter's voice? Would she ever forget the unbelieving vindictive look that Sara had given her when, hair tumbled, gown gaping open on her full bosom, Sara had arisen to stare unbelievingly up at Peter and then had turned to face Tiffany? Behind her, mouth agape, was Sara's lover, naked to the waist. An instant later, he had vaulted the wall, pushed Peter down, jumped back, and seizing the gasping, sobbing Sara by the hand, had fled into the woods.

Tiffany had knelt by the fallen man. "Are you hurt?" she had cried.

His eyes, dazed at first, had fastened on her face. "You knew!" Catching her arm in a hurtful grip, he accused her.

"Yes, I h-heard them making plans to meet here . . ." she had faltered at anger that seemed directed at her. "I thought you ought to know."

"Did you?" he had snarled. "Get away from me, you misbegotten little sneak, I do not want to look at you . . ."

Peter had hated Tiffany that night five years ago. Would he understand now that she had done the deed because she loved him?

Novels by
Zabrina Faire

Enchanting Jenny
Lady Blue
The Midnight Match
The Romany Rebel
The Wicked Cousin
Athena's Airs
Bold Pursuit
Pretty Kitty
Tiffany's True Love

Published by
WARNER BOOKS

Your Warner Library of Regency Romance

Tiffany's True Love

Zabrina Faire

WARNER BOOKS

A Warner Communications Company

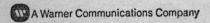

One

"Taffy is a Welchman.
Taffy is a thief!
Taffy came to our house
And stole a leg o' beef."

Tom Prine chanted the verse loudly.

Tiffany stiffened, hating the song, hating her step-brother, hating the nickname Sir Matthew Prine had given her—she did not know why, for she was not Welsh. Yet both Tom and his father insisted on dubbing her Taffy—though Sir Matthew, of course, did not burst into song whenever he saw her, or tease her or pull her hair or play frightening pranks upon her. Generally, he ignored her, which she preferred far more than when he did deign to recognize her existence. Her hand stole up to her face.

"You're going to the Jews this afternoon," Tom jeered. "And you might never come back—for they dine on Christian flesh!"

She lifted her chin. "I am going visiting with Mama."

"To the Jews."

"To Mama's cousin Peter Medina. He is—"

"A Jew, a Jew, a Jew," Tom yelled.

"He is the Master of Clive Abbey," she dared to correct.

"And all the Clives whirling in their graves!" Tom chortled.

He was quoting his father, of course. Sir Matthew's words came back to her. They had followed fast upon Mama's mentioning her Cousin Ellen, Peter's mother. "She was very kind to me when I was younger," she murmured.

"You'd much in common," Sir Matthew had commented dryly. "Birds of a feather, my dear. Ellen Clive eloping with her Jew music teacher and you . . ." He had laughed. "Lord, between the two of you, you've about done for the toplofty Clives. I imagine the lot of 'em're whirling in their graves. It's a wonder they can stay put in the churchyard—a Jew in residence at Clive Abbey! That, I imagine, is the bitterest pill to gulp."

Mama had firmed her lips and refrained from answering Sir Matthew—refrained from reminding him that it was at his insistence that she was going to see Peter Medina. It had to do with their current situation which, Tom had informed Tiffany, could not be worse. "We're in the basket and that's a fact. It could be the Fleet."

Tiffany had not needed to ask her mother to explain Tom's statement. She had only to look about her at their lodgings—three squalid rooms at the top of a narrow house in a part of town which Mama called "dreadful." They had moved there recently. It was their fourth move in two years. Just after Mama and Sir Matthew had been wed, they had lived in a handsome little mansion off St. James Square. But Sir Matthew had had the "devil's own luck" at the tables, and they had changed to a less prestigious address but still a pleasant house with servants, though not as many as before. By the time of the third move, the servants had gone and the house had been

6

exchanged for rooms at the edge of Mayfair; their current lodgings were dangerously close to the slums of Covent Garden. Earlier in the week, Mrs. Bowes, their landlady, had appeared in the outer hall, her beady eyes alight with rage, as she screamed at Mama about what was owed her. She had shrilled about "them wot thinks they're better'n the lot o' us an' 'aven't two farthings to rub against each other," mentioning debtor's prison and bailiffs, and threatening to have the latter on them if she did not get her money in a matter of three days. She would have had considerably more to say to frighten shrinking Lady Mary had not Sir Matthew suddenly rounded on her, threatening to throw her "ugly carcass" down the stairs if she did not "stow her gab."

That encounter had been followed by another of the increasingly frequent quarrels between Mama and Sir Matthew. Mama had decried the loss of her huge dowry which she had accused him of wasting in hells. As usual, he had come back with the puzzling retort that she was lucky any honest man would bestow his name on her and her brat; to which Mama, rather than dissolving into tears as she usually did, had answered that it was a high price to pay for a low name and that she had been better off with her first husband, the Irish officer who had died before her daughter's birth.

Sir Matthew had raised his hand as if to strike her, but oddly enough, he had turned and begun to strike Tiffany about the face and chest. Mama had burst out weeping, and somehow out of this strange argument it had been decided that the very next day, she would go to visit her Cousin Peter or, as her stepfather preferred to describe him, "the Jew."

Tiffany touched her face. It was still sore—her eye was blackened and there was a raised welt on her cheekbone. However, she had not wept at the hurt. In the two years that she had lived in Sir Matthew's house, she had often been beaten, generally for no particular reason. In the beginning, she had wept—but then she had been a mere baby, only ten. Once she had turned eleven, she had discovered that it gave her stepfather a certain satisfac-

7

tion to witness her pain. He always smiled after he had administered a particularly cruel blow. Hating him as she did, she had no wish to add to his pleasure. She had discovered it was surprisingly easy to refrain from weeping, particularly since this attitude confounded and infuriated him.

She stifled a sigh. It would have been so much easier if he had not been there. Though it was futile to remember when there had been just Mama and herself living with Cousin Anne, she did think wistfully of it. Oddly enough, she had not cared much for Cousin Anne either. She conjured up a picture of her—she had been quite tall and thin with a sallow complexion, hard narrow eyes and a long nose. She had looked down that nose at Tiffany, shaking her head while breathing words concerning folly and lost opportunities. At such times, Mama had burst into tears. Still, it had been infinitely more comfortable before Sir Matthew had come into their lives. Tiffany remembered when he had appeared—introduced to Mama by an old friend of Cousin Anne, a Mr. Brinkley. Tiffany had disliked him from the first even though Cousin Anne had disconcertingly referred to him as a "godsend" and Mama had blushed prettily whenever James, Cousin Anne's elderly butler, had ushered him into her small drawing room. Neither lady had seemed to mind his loud hectoring voice, his brandy-scented breath and his small sharp brown eyes which were set too close to his nose. Once he had brought Tom, aged eleven, who was even more unprepossessing in appearance—a shock of fiery red hair and skin blotched with big reddish freckles. Tiffany, a shy nine-soon-to-be-ten, had shrunk from him when he had rendered his features even uglier by surreptitiously making horrid faces at her. Subsequently, he had tweaked her long curls so viciously that she had cried out loud, annoying and embarrassing Mama, who had forthwith sent her to bed.

In those days, Sir Matthew had the reputation of being a young man of fortune—a Corinthian, Mama had said admiringly. He had enjoyed the friendship of the Prince Regent, who was known to consult him on the buying of racehorses. However, once he had wed Mama, he complained that this same friendship had ended, and muttered that he knew from which direction the ill wind had blown. He had stared at Tiffany in a very odd manner—and soon after that, Tom had started singing the ditty which annoyed her so much—"Taffy is a Welshman." From being called Tiffany, she became Taffy to everyone except Mama. Mama had been equally annoyed at this particular change of name, but when she had remonstrated with her new husband, he had laughed and said mockingly, "I happen to think it particularly apt, my dear Mary."

Mama had wept and fled from the room.

Thinking about all of this, the child was confused. Throughout her short life, she had been aware that something was wrong with her, but no one had actually told her what it was—not Cousin Anne, not Sir Matthew, not even Tom. Yet it was there and . . .

"Tiffany, my love."

Tiffany's uncomfortable recollections fled as she turned to face a small, slight young woman in a white muslin gown. The resemblance between the two of them was immediately apparent. Both were fair, with curling golden hair, straight lovely noses and oval faces. However, Tiffany's eyes were larger than those of her mother and deep blue rather than gray. There was a tilt to them and more fullness about the mouth. Her chin bore a cleft and it was firmer than her mother's. Indeed, there was less vulnerability in the child's face, though Mary Prine was fully thirty years old and had had more than her portion of sorrow, she stared about her with the wide, wondering gaze of a young girl.

"Mama, you do look so beautiful!" Tiffany breathed.

"Do I?" Lady Mary spoke apprehensively. Her gray eyes darkened as she regarded her daughter. "Oh dear, your poor eye . . . does it hurt?"

"Not in the least, Mama. I do not let it hurt me," Tiffany retorted fiercely.

"You do not let it . . ." The gray eyes were suddenly

wet. "Oh, it is all wrong ... who would have believed ... But we must not speak about such things, else I shall be in a wretched mood, even more than I am already, having to ... If it were not for— But no, I must not even think of ... thoughts can plague one so dreadfully."

"Can they indeed, dear Mary?"

Mother and daughter whirled as Sir Matthew strolled into the room. He was wearing his brocade dressing gown. It had been a handsome garment when it was first made, but it was shabby now and stained at cuffs and lapels. His hair was tousled and there was a two-day-old beard upon a countenance which was flushed with the brandy he had been drinking all morning. His speech was slurred and his eyes bleary as they rested upon the childish figure of his wife.

"And what manner of dreadful thoughts are plaguing you? Are you yet so averse to visiting your Jew cousin? Goes against your pride, does it?" He stepped to her side and reaching out, he cupped his hand around her chin, seemingly unaware of her hasty step backward. "Pride, my dearest love, is an expense neither you nor I can afford."

Lady Mary shook off his hand. "I did not mean ..." she began defensively.

"Be damned to you," he said roughly. "I don't care what you meant. Mind you get a good sum from him. Weep, my love. He'll not be proof against the sight of those drowned orbs. There's no female who cries as prettily as you. Practice makes perfect. And tell him how I beat the brat—that should bring in another gratuity. 'Tis said that the Israelites are particularly fond of children."

"Oh, I pray you, enough." Lady Mary spoke in a low voice.

He was at her side again, his hands heavy on her shoulders as he glared down at her. "Enough, is it? I've half a mind to— But no, I shan't strike you. You must needs look your best. Your best and her worst. The contrast will bring in the gold. Get along with you now." He gave her a little shove.

Tiffany did not breathe until they had come out of the door downstairs into the tiny cul-de-sac of a street. Then, seeing her mother's tremulous smile and quick blinking of tear-tipped lashes, she said in one of her fierce whispers, "I pray you'll not weep, Mama."

Meeting her daughter's steady gaze, Lady Mary swallowed and shook her head. "No, I shall not. Oh God, I wish I need not see him. He will tell Ellen and she— Oh, if there were only some way . . . someone. He had such address and I thought . . ." Apologetically she regarded Tiffany. "He did seem so attentive and I was lonely and your father being d-dead, but it was only the money and now it's all gone . . . everything."

Tiffany put a thin hand on her mother's arm. "Do not think on it, Mama. Let us go. He is probably watching from above."

Lady Mary, sending a frightened glance in the direction of the attic windows, stiffened. "He is," she whispered. "Come, then." She lifted her skirts above the filthy street and ran as fast as she might from the gaze of those watchful eyes.

The drawing room of the Clive mansion on Berkeley Square was hung in gold silk and, with a few exceptions, its furniture was French, imported from Paris fifty years earlier by Sir Bertram Clive. An Aubusson carpet, gold to match the draperies, lay on the floor and an ormolu clock ticked on a marble mantelpiece. Over the clock was Sir Joshua Reynolds's portrait of Ellen Clive. It had been painted when she was sixteen, a year before she had eloped with Esdras Medina and two years before the birth of her only child—Peter. The painting depicted a pretty, fair-haired girl with gentle gray eyes and a vulnerable mouth.

Occasionally when Peter Medina glanced at the portrait, he thought his mother had changed very little in the ensuing twenty-five years. At forty-one, she was still fair and the mouth was still vulnerable. He regarded it now with a mixture of affection and exasperation. If . . . but he refused to dwell on that "if" and all the other "if's" that plagued him. He had a visitor whom Carter, who had admitted him a moment earlier, obviously thought sadly out of place in that magnificent chamber. That this was also the opinion of Herr Louis Horvath, a small, shabbily dressed old man, was equally evident. Cradling a violin case in his arms, he stood near one of the damask-covered Louis XV chairs, ignoring his host's invitation to be seated. With an eagerness edged with triumph, he said in a soft, Hungarian-accented tone, "After last night, I had to bring this to you, Peter . . . or should I say Simon Esdras?"

"You must say Peter. Simon Esdras is a secret that we share," Peter said firmly.

"The whole world should share that secret. You should not need to hide such gold beneath straw." Horvath's eyes were sad. "Nor should you give your music only to a few. In Vienna . . . in St. Petersburg . . . in every great music capital of the world you should play."

"I think you grow extravagant, Louis."

"If your father were to hear you, he would say the same. If—"

"You said you had something to show me, Louis. I need not ask what it is. But I must tell you, too, that I am most satisfied with the Amati you found for me two years ago. It is the finest instrument I have ever possessed."

"The Amati is very well," Horvath dismissed. "But this . . ." He freed one hand from the case to make a sweeping gesture. "A Stradivarius, Peter. Made by the first Stradivari—Antonio, not his sons."

"Ah!" An eager light now shone from Peter's eyes. Moving to a table on which were a number of objects d'art, he unceremoniously pushed aside a malachite box, a Dresden shepherdess and a small bronze Apollo. "Show it to me, then."

Placing the case gently on the table, the man opened it and stood back with an air of triumph. "It was once owned by the Archduke Victor of Saxony, whose ancestor had it from the son of its maker. Until very recently, it was the property of the late Sebastian Hagar. His widow sold it to me."

"A fine artist." Lifting the violin from its case, he ran a slender finger over its strings. Tucking the instrument under his chin, he took the bow from the case and played a few tentative chords. Then, making some adjustments to the strings, he performed a cadenza.

"Ah . . ." Horvath's reverence shifted subtly from instrument to performer. "The sound . . . the sound. If I were to shut my eyes, I should think it was your father—and you have even more dexterity. And last night, in that wretched little hall . . . Four months ago, in Naples, I heard Paganini play. I was ready to fall on my knees, for indeed he was kissed by the muse and she has kissed you too, Peter—kissed and blessed you and—"

"Please," Peter said returning the violin to its case, "you know my problems."

"I know, too, that they are not insurmountable."

"I have a responsibility to my mother and to my fiancée . . . and the Abbey."

"You have a responsibility to the memory of your father . . . and to this violin."

"I have not said I will purchase it. I should not purchase it, Louis. It is folly for me to have it. By rights, it should belong to another Hagar or a Spohr or a Paganini."

"But you will buy it," Horvath said positively.

"Yes." Peter looked at the old man with some exasperation. "I should have stuffed my ears with wax before I heard your siren's song. Yet—I can hardly believe that the price you quoted is enough."

Herr Horvath breathed a sigh of relief. "It is enough, and Esdras would have wanted you to have it."

"It was he who should have possessed it." Peter smiled bitterly. "He was the virtuoso."

"You have surpassed him. It is a great pity—"

Peter held up his slender musician's hand. "Please." Taking a purse from his pocket, he counted out a number of gold pieces and pressed them into Horvath's hand.

"This is more than—" he protested.

"Enough, Louis. There should be no price affixed to the priceless."

Horvath stuttered his thanks and was gone. Peter looked gloomily at the violin, wondering what Louis would have said had he known that Conrad Melchior, the famed manager, had approached him offering a series of concerts in Vienna for the following fall. He had been amazed and angered at the refusal. Peter sighed. Impulsively he picked up the violin and began to play a short sonata by Tartini, stopping as he felt rather than saw Carter, his valet, in the doorway. "Well?" he demanded impatiently.

Carter, a slim man with a bland expression in his pale blue eyes, said deferentially, "Lady Mary Prine and Miss Tiffany Prine have arrived, sir."

"Ah." Peter reluctantly replaced the violin in its case and shut the lid. "I had forgotten. Show Lady Mary—" He paused. "Miss Tiffany?"

"A little girl, sir," the valet clarified.

"Oh, yes." Peter nodded, remembering the child and all his mother had told him about her. He even had a vague memory of her as a babe-in-arms, some eleven years back when he had had a disdain for babies and perhaps a jealousy too, watching Ellen leaning over Tiffany's cradle. Catching Carter's glance, he said quickly, "Show them in, please."

The valet turned away and then, surprisingly, turned back. "The . . . er, child, sir," he began. Suddenly flushing, he said with something less than his usual sangfroid, "Excuse me, sir." He moved out quickly, leaving Peter to wonder at Carter's incipient confidence. Equally unsettling had been Lady Mary's note asking if she might see him. It had been the first word he had received from her in over a decade. Fully ten years had passed since she had left the abbey and in those days, she had taken very little notice of his fourteen-year-old self. Of course, she had been much troubled. At Ellen's invitation, she had come to the abbey to bear her child and though his mother had pressed her to stay, she had left when her baby was a year old, preferring, she had explained, to go back to her Cousin Anne in London.

Ellen Clive Medina had not believed that particular

14

excuse; Peter had heard her discussing it with Hannah, her abigail, a trusted confidante. She had said something about Mary not wanting to remain in places she had known as a child. He had not understood that then. He did now, but he still did not know why she wanted to see him. The few surviving members of the Clive family—all female—were not desirous of either renewing or making his acquaintance. His lip curled at this thought, and it was with that saturnine expression on his face that Tiffany, entering a step behind her mother, first saw her second cousin. She halted abruptly, staring at him in surprise.

She had been more than a little afraid of him, she realized. Her stepfather's sneers concerning his ancestry would not normally have disturbed her, but even in her short life, she had heard enough mutterings from servants—even from Mrs. Bowes—to realize that Jews were considered sinister and evil. They were not like Christian folk—they banded together to cheat and rob them. Once she had heard her stepfather mutter about one Isaac Levy, who had exacted his full "pound of flesh" from an unfortunate friend. Others of his acquaintance called the whole race a "pack of bloodsuckers." She had also heard that particular term used by the various young men who had visited Cousin Anne's house; certainly that sharp-tongued lady had spoken disparagingly about Ellen Clive's scandalous elopement with her music teacher, marveling that her father had taken her back after her husband's untimely death, eight years later. That had been bad enough—but what had been even worse was his settling Clive Abbey, its extensive lands and a great part of his fortune on his grandson.

"I shudder to think of one of that wretched race being installed at the Abbey. If he had none of his own, Sir Arthur should have thought of one of his wife's relations. I do not mean myself—but there are others—Gerald, for instance."

"Sir Gerald has his own estate and fortune," Lady Mary had said mildly.

"It would have been far more fitting, nonetheless.

15

Imagine that Medina cub at the Abbey. It curdles my blood!"

Confronted with that "Medina cub," the child could only gaze openmouthed at the most handsome man she ever remembered seeing. He was tall and dark-haired, and since his skin was a warm olive, it seemed that he should have had brown eyes rather than silver gray. Set under winged black brows, they had just the suggestion of a slant. His nose was slightly aquiline and his mouth particularly appealing, well-shaped and firm above a chin cleft like her own. If his hair waved riotously over his broad forehead, his dress was neat. In fact, he must have absorbed Beau Brummel's stern dicta on masculine attire, for rather than the ostentatious garments which Tom insisted were favored by the Israelites—diamond rings on every finger and a flock of gold fobs at their waists—her cousin's coat was of gray superfine and his cravat, though intricately tied, boasted no pearl studs, nor were there rings on his long, slim fingers. The only gold he wore glinted from the tassels of his highly polished Hessian boots, the fob at his waist being merely dark leather.

"Tiffany." There was an edge to her mother's tone. "Will you not give your cousin Peter a greeting?"

She flushed, aware now that he was looking at her and that he must have spoken to her. She curtseyed and gave him a shy smile. "I am indeed glad to meet you, cousin," she murmured.

He had no answering smile for her. In his mind were Carter's few words on the subject of the child. He knew now that the man had remarked her bruised face and swollen eye. There was censure in the gaze he bent on her mother. "I should rather believe that those injuries were caused by a fall—but from their nature, I cannot."

Lady Mary winced. "It was not a fall," she acknowledged in a low voice. "It was why I—I could not leave her at home."

"Good God!" he exclaimed. "No one should treat a little girl in such a manner. Can you not prevent it?"

Tears appeared in Lady Mary's eyes. "You do n-not understand," she faltered.

16

Tiffany, seeing her mother's shame, ran to her side and cast protective arms about her. Giving Peter one of her fierce glances, she cried imperiously, "Leave her alone. It's not her fault and besides I was not hurt!"

The tenseness of the moment was dissolved by Peter's laughter. "Now, there's spirit!"

"Too much . . . too much," her mother moaned. "I fear for her, cousin. She is too brave and . . ."

"Is she?" His silver gaze rested on Tiffany once more. "And given that very evident spirit, there's no silencing her, I should think."

"Not when she believes herself my defender," Lady Mary agreed ruefully.

"She, she, she. I do wish you'd not speak as if I were not present," Tiffany complained.

His laughter was once more in her ears. "You do well to dislike such talk, child. I did, too, at your age." His face hardened. "I grew used to it, however. It happened often enough as it must with—" He broke off and turned back to Lady Mary. "Her stepfather?" he inquired curtly.

"He resents . . ."

"Can you not intervene . . ." Yet before she could answer, evidently summing up her yielding nature, he continued, "Is there no place she might be sent? A friend . . ."

Lady Mary's glance shifted to the floor. Studying part of the pattern in the carpet, she said, "I have no friends. My cousin Anne's removed to Scotland and besides . . ."

"No, that would not suffice." He grimaced. "My mother might help."

"Cousin Ellen?" Lady Mary said disbelievingly.

"She loves children. Five years ago, she took in Sara Wingfield when her parents succumbed to a virulent fever."

"The Wingfields." Lady Mary looked distressed. "I'd not heard. Is she quite alone then?"

His expressive eyes glowed. "She is not alone."

"I meant . . . I believed she had an elder brother."

"Charles is fighting on the Peninsula."

"Is he of such an age? Sara must yet be very young."

"Near nineteen and Charles is twenty-two." Diffidently he added, "Sara and I are betrothed. We shall be wed when Charles has his next leave—which should be soon."

Lady Mary put out her hand. "I do wish you happy."

Taking it, he held it for a moment. "I thank you. I . . . we are very—very happy."

Tiffany frowned. Though she could not have explained why she had felt an immediate antipathy to Miss Sara Wingfield!

"However," Peter was continuing, "we are from the subject. My mother would, I know, receive Cousin Tiffany with great pleasure—if you could find it in your heart to let her come for a visit."

"A visit," she repeated apprehensively. "H-how long a visit?"

"Two to three months?"

"No, I could not leave Mama," Tiffany cried, edging closer to Lady Mary.

"Hush, child," her mother said with more sternness than usual. "Two to three months. But your mother might not—"

"She would be delighted."

"It might be an answer," Lady Mary murmured. "Two to three months is not a long time." She fixed a yearning look upon her daughter, running a gentle hand through her curls.

"Mama, you must not think of it. What would you do?"

"How often have you questioned me about the Abbey, dearest. Should you not like to see it?"

"Not unless you come with me."

Lady Mary seemed to be swallowing a painful obstruction in her throat. Then, she said with a tentative smile, "But I will come *for* you, dearest." She darted a

18

glance at Peter. "And it may be that I will stay a week with Cousin Ellen."

"No!" Tiffany stamped her foot.

"Tiffany!" Lady Mary shook her head. "Will you disgrace me utterly? Peter will think I have taught you nothing of manners."

Usually such a reprimand from her mother silenced the child, but this time she went on stubbornly. "I shall not go! What would you do when he . . . he . . ."

Lady Mary was visited by inspiration. "It is quite possible that it would be easier for me if—if you were to be away briefly, my own."

"Easier?" the child repeated.

"We . . . Matthew and I have been quite compatible when you . . . well, when we had not to live in each other's shadow, as it were. The four of us in those small lodgings. Naturally, 'tis not easy for any of us and Matthew has an uncertain temper. If you were not there—" She broke off, quailing at Tiffany's wide, agonized stare.

"You do not want me to be with you anymore, Mama?"

"Love, of course, I want it. But for a little while . . . three months only . . ."

Tiffany, paling, turned her face away. In a smothered voice, she accused, "You do not want me anymore."

"My dearest." Lady Mary stretched out her arms ready to gather her daughter into them, ready to murmur that she had not meant it, but even as she moved in her direction, she caught Peter's eyes. He was mouthing something and she realized he was saying, "Let her believe what she will." With a deep sigh, she gave him a tiny nod and let her arms fall to her sides.

With a determination foreign to her, she said, "I think, my dear child, that if your cousins will have you for three months, it would be better for all concerned."

Hearing the decision in Lady Mary's voice, Tiffany was filled with despair. Blinking back her threatening

19

tears, she looked from her mother to Peter Medina. Both were so much older than herself. Obviously, they were in league against her—talking down to her, calling her a "child." It would be of little use to tell them that she did not feel a child—not since she had turned twelve. Even before that, she had appointed herself the protector of her mother. Had her efforts to shield Lady Mary from her stepfather's wrath served only to inflame him against her—against them both? It was very possible. She was courageous enough to admit that.

She cast her mind back to the time when they had lived in the large houses and there had been servants to tend her and a governess, rather than her mother, to teach her her letters. It was a dimming memory, but she did recall that in those days Sir Matthew had not lifted his hand against her—and not even Tom had been so horrid. Had she herself been at the root of her mother's trouble? Again she felt the prick of tears and ruthlessly blinked them away. Her mother's weeping never accomplished anything beyond curses or jeers from Sir Matthew. She tensed. Lady Mary was picking up her reticule and glancing toward the door!

Was she on the point of bidding farewell to their cousin? She could not—not yet! Their reason for visiting him was not to discuss a stay at the Abbey. There had been another, much more pressing reason for their call and that had not yet been revealed to their host. From her knowledge of Lady Mary's timorous ways as well as her reluctance to discuss such vulgar subjects as debts, she feared it would not be broached!

"Mama," she mouthed.

Lady Mary was not looking in her direction. Predictably, she was saying, "Well, Cousin, I fear we have remained far too long and—"

"Mama!" Tiffany cried.

"My dear?" Lady Mary looked at her reproachfully. "You forget the manners I have been at such pains to teach you. You must not interrupt. Whatever will your Cousin Peter think of you?"

"I assure you—" he began.

"Mama," Tiffany prompted shrilly. "The Fleet!"

Lady Mary gave her a blank stare. "The . . . the Fleet?" Knowledge leaped into her eyes and she blushed crimson, staring down at the floor. "We . . . oh, dear," she moaned. "I wish . . . but . . ."

"Are you in danger of debtor's prison?" he demanded.

As Lady Mary toyed with the strings of her reticule, Tiffany cried, "Yes, yes, yes! The woman who owns the house where we lodge has threatened to send bailiffs. She is horrid, she yells at poor Mama when 'tis Sir Matthew—"

"Tiffany!" Lady Mary shook her head. Ashamedly she added, "I—I'd not have come to you, dear P-Peter, but 'twas none else we could ask and h-hearing from a friend that you were in residence . . . I . . ."

He put a hand on her arm, telling her gently, "I pray you will say no more. I am only pleased that you have come and that I am made aware that you are in want. If you will accompany me into the library, I shall give you a draught on my bank."

"Oh, oh, dear," Lady Mary whispered, dabbing at her eyes with a tiny scrap of cambric. "You are so good. You see Matthew has had dreadful luck at the tables."

"He never wins," Tiffany said.

"Oh, he does, dear. He has on dogs and . . . it's only horses . . ."

"And dice," Tiffany reminded her knowledgeably.

"Yes, but—Peter, if—if Matthew's luck were to . . . return. He did have some very good days at The Two Sevens, I think it's called . . . though lately, but it could—"

"Come," he interrupted. "Do not speak of that. Anything I give you must be considered a gift, not a loan."

Tiffany, whose initially good impression of her relative had changed into anger at his interfering ways, made a sudden and overwhelming discovery—the ramifications

21

of which she did not entirely understand at the moment. Its first expression was in the bright, glowing smile that she turned on him and which he, still regarding Lady Mary concernedly, did not see.

Two

Staring out the coach window, Tiffany watched a single raindrop course down, splitting the glass in half. Another flurry of drops erased the illusion and blurred the yellow fields. Beyond them, there was the sea, luminously purple and pink from such rays of the sun as escaped through slits in the lowering gray clouds. The sky was nearly all gray, but surprisingly some of the thunderheads were edged with a froth of paler mist which reminded her of lace on one of her mother's ball gowns. Below, grassy cliffs reared up over the sea. The land seemed surprisingly barren. They had not passed any human habitation for hours—only vast green or golden fields and hills crowned with thick masses of trees. Grazing cattle, however, were everywhere and several times Joseph, their coachman, had halted to allow flocks of sheep to cross the road. Though she had often witnessed these same peregrinations in London, she had never seen so many of the animals. To the city-bred child, the contrast between noisy packed streets and the vast emptiness of the countryside was startling. Of course, they had passed through small villages with houses huddling against each other, but they were riding on the deserted lanes again seemingly in minutes. Occasionally, the monotony would be broken by skeletons of ancient castles perched on high hills. Some of these battered edifices had been identified for her by her cousin. He had also pointed out sites where historical events had taken place. In the last few hours, however, he had fallen silent, staring out of his window, his long fingers absently sliding up and down the violin case he had held protectively on his lap throughout the journey.

Tiffany, instructed by her mother to speak only when addressed by him, had refrained from questioning him about the case—though she had wondered at the strange, almost sorrowful glances he had cast at it from time to time. There was much about him that puzzled her. When she had first met him, he had seemed no different from any of the young men who had visited them in the days when her mother and stepfather had still received their friends. The difference became apparent to her only after they had been closeted together in the coach.

Peter Medina was a man of moods and all of them were easily discernible—emotions of pleasure, anger, joy, and frustration passed like cloud shadows over his mobile countenance. He had none of the impassive calm that characterized her stepfather and his cronies. He was also incredibly sensitive to her moods and so gentle—so unlike Sir Matthew and Tom that it did not seem as if they could inhabit the same world!

She wished she might banish all thoughts of her stepfather and brother, but that was impossible. In the week that had elapsed before Peter had come to fetch her, Sir Matthew had been actually affable—his good temper stemming in part from the large sum her mother had obtained from the man he still insisted upon terming her "Jew-cousin." However, he was equally pleased at the invitation that would relieve him of her presence, at least for the next three months. He had even agreed that some part of their money must be used to provide Tiffany with new garments. Fortunately, muslin was cheap and Lady Mary was clever with her needle. In an amazingly short time, she had fashioned several becoming gowns for the little girl and a new cloak of thick wool. "It'll be much colder up north," Lady Mary had explained, "even in early August, and the house is large. There are many chill corners. You must always remember to stay close to the fire, else you will catch cold."

Tiffany, who had never heard Lady Mary mention the house, had plied her with eager questions, but beyond telling her that it had considerable grounds of its own and lay on a cliff between York and the seaport town of Whitby, she had said little else. Knowing her mother as well as she did, Tiffany had the notion that it pained her to discuss it. Thinking on it, she could remember only one time when Lady Mary had said much about her past. They had been walking at the edge of Hyde Park and on seeing a crested coach pass, Lady Mary had cried, "Oh, there's Lady Katherine Broughton—she is a particular friend of Queen Charlotte. The Queen had wanted her as a lady-in-waiting, so Phoebe told me, but she was too much in awe of the King. He could be disconcerting. I remember his appearing suddenly in the palace corridor, staring straight at me and crying, 'What, what, what!' I was frightened to death and Phoebe said it was quite usual and he would never harm anyone, poor man."

"Oh, Mama, you must have been at court! And who was Phoebe?"

Lady Mary had paled and shaken her head. "No, child, I was never at court—save that once. Phoebe was a friend . . . oh, look, the swans. Six of them. Or are they ducks over there on the Serpentine? Shall we watch them, darling?" She had hurried away so quickly that Tiffany had had trouble keeping up with her and since Lady Mary had talked only about the swans or rather ducks, as indeed they were, it had been impossible to mention the court again . . . or the mysterious Phoebe.

She sighed. They were far, far from Lady Mary—miles and miles and months. As always when she thought of her mother, tears threatened, but she would not shed them. Furthermore, much as she regretted leaving Lady Mary, she could not weep over the separation from Sir Matthew and Tom. *Tom.* She shuddered and gritted her teeth. He had played one more horrible, ghastly trick on her that week, but she did not want to dwell on it for she had to remember that she had acted like the merest baby, crying, shrieking, begging him to come back to her and hearing only silence. With an effort, she pushed that memory out of her mind only to fill it with another which was also distressing—the final moments of leave-taking.

It had been an exciting morning—exciting and confusing with everyone rushing hither and thither and Mrs. Bowes impressed by the shining equipage and the four matched grays which had drawn up on their miserable street. Half the neighborhood had come out to admire them and the whores who prowled the street had paraded in front of the smartly dressed coachman, footman and postboys. In spite of his prejudices, Sir Matthew had been very courteous to Peter Medina—almost exaggeratedly so, Tiffany had thought—while Tom had hung back, eyeing him resentfully. She herself had been excited, too. Though her mother had told her she had been born at the Abbey and lived there for a year, naturally her memory did not stretch back that far. Consequently she had been caught between eagerness to see the estate and grief at leaving Mama—even if Mama did not want her to stay and would be more comfortable without her. So when Lady Mary had embraced her, it had been a shock to feel her arms so tight about her and to find her mother's eyes red-rimmed and her face deadly pale. In that instant, she knew that all her mother had said about wanting her away had been untrue. Preternaturally sensitive to all of her mother's moods, she divined that Lady Mary would miss her dreadfully. In a sense, this certainty carried some grains of comfort; it had hurt her sorely to believe that her mother's life would be more peaceful if she were away. However, in another sense, she had longed to beg Peter not to take her away—but that, of course, was impossible. Such a request would not only be unmannerly, it would be unheeded. She must remember that in their eyes she was a child—and, of course, there had been that incident with Tom that had proved her more babyish than she had thought herself to be.

"Tiffany." Peter's hand rested lightly on her arm. "We are turning into the grounds."

She was glad to be diverted from the uncomfortable thoughts buzzing through her head. Eagerly, she looked out of the window only to see masses of trees growing close to the side of a narrowed road, their leaves beginning to fade and the tangled weeds beneath them turned a late summer yellow. In a few moments, however, they had passed a stone gatehouse with a man standing in front of it. He was big and burly with a red face marked with smile lines, but his expression seemed dour and unwelcoming. The road before them became winding, then finally it straightened out and after some twenty minutes, they came into a clearing centered by a massive gray stone mansion, its facade punctuated by tall narrow windows and its roof flat and protected by a stone railing. A wide expanse of clipped grass lay before it and aged trees grew all around. Though it was a larger house than most of those she had seen in London, she was disappointed. She had expected it must bear some likeness to a church.

"Is this an abbey, then, cousin?" she inquired.

"No, though it bears the name. The house was built at the beginning of the last century to replace an older mansion erected at the beginning of Queen Elizabeth's reign and burned down in 1699. The original abbey was destroyed in 1540 and the grounds ceded to my ancestor, who had marked it as his own before the dissolution of the monasteries. Do you know about that, my dear?"

"Oh, yes," she replied glibly. "King Henry divorced his first wife and became head of the church."

He smiled. "A neat way of summing it up. There

27

are, you will be happy to know, some remains of the original edifice. They are out on the grounds. Once you're settled, I shall show them to you."

"Oh," she said, her eyes gleaming, "I should like that."

During this brief exchange, the post chaise had drawn to a stop and the footman had opened the door. Clutching his outstretched arm, she descended the steps he had placed there for her convenience. In that same moment, she saw that the oaken door at the front of the house had been flung wide. A plump, fair-haired woman in a blue muslin gown came hurrying out just as Peter, alighting, called. "I hope you received my letter, Mama."

"I did, my love," she responded, as she joined them. She embraced him and then smiled down at the child. "And this is Tiffany," she said warmly. "You have a great look of Mary," she observed, with an odd note of relief in her voice. "It will be delightful having you here again, but I do not expect you remember me. Oh, of course you could not. You were scarcely a year old when you left. I do wish your mama could have returned with you. Perhaps one day, she will."

"I do not know, ma'am." Tiffany curtseyed.

"Ma'am!" Ellen Medina's rich laughter was in her ears. "I vow you must not call me 'ma'am.' I am your Cousin Ellen and—" She broke off, staring at the violin case Peter was carrying. Her brows drew together. "Another violin, my dear?" she demanded in a strained tone.

"A Stradivarius, Mother."

Watching her Cousin Ellen, Tiffany discerned a look of anxiety mixed with pain, but it was quickly gone, replaced by a bright smile. "A Stradivarius! Oh, then I *do* understand! A very fine instrument, is it not?"

"Very fine," he agreed. He looked about him. "Sara . . . where is she?"

"She's gone riding, my love. She left early. She said she hoped to meet your carriage and ride back with you. I am surprised, she did not—ah, but here she comes."

The sound of hooves was in Tiffany's ears as a girl

on horseback came around a bend in the driveway. Though she was dressed in a neat dark habit, her hat must have fallen off for her hair was a tangle of red gold locks, which clustered about her face. Bringing her steed to a halt, she dismounted hastily, throwing the reins to Joseph, who still lingered by the post chaise. She sped toward Peter and, oblivious of anyone else, clutched his arm possessively, saying in soft, slightly husky tones, "Oh, you were cruel to remain so long in town. Have you no heart—or perhaps you think I have none?"

"Sara, love." He flushed and there was no mistaking the adoration in his eyes. "I came as soon as I might."

Tiffany felt a wave of resentment wash over her. She remembered her instant antipathy when he had first mentioned his fiancée. Seeing the girl, she found it had increased—which was very confusing. She was very pretty, with the white skin common to redheads and a slim lovely figure. Certainly there was no reason to dislike Sara, but Tiffany was conscious of an overwhelming desire to push her away from Peter. It was particularly embarrassing that Sara should take notice of her at that particular moment.

"And this must be our little guest," she observed in a tone which made Tiffany feel as if she were six rather than twelve.

"Yes, this is our Cousin Tiffany," Ellen confirmed. "My dear"—she gave her another lovely smile—"this is Miss Sara Wingfield, who will soon be your cousin, too."

"My cousin?" Tiffany looked purposely confused.

"Peter and I are betrothed." Sara smiled. "And shall be wed directly my brother comes to give us his blessing." Sara directed a warm glance at Peter and then stared down at the child out of eyes which were as green as grass. "I am delighted to meet you," she continued, "even if you kept my darling from me for a full week longer than he'd promised." Without waiting for a comment, she turned back to Peter. "But you must have news of the court, too. The *on dit* here is that Brummel dared to turn his back on the Prince and called him fat to his face."

Tiffany giggled. "How might he turn his back on

him and call him fat to his face at the same time?" she inquired reasonably.

Peter laughed. "It would require a supple figure— more supple than even the lissome Beau possesses, I'm thinking."

Sara's green eyes glinted. " 'Twas what I heard," she replied sulkily.

"It did not happen quite that way." Peter smiled at her indulgently. " 'Twas the Prince who turned his back on Brummel, who is said to have inquired of Lord Alvanley, 'Who's your fat friend?' "

"Oh!" Ellen clapped her hands. "I hope he said it loudly."

"Evidently he said it loudly enough to have it trumpeted through London and the countryside as well," Peter observed dryly.

"I hold no brief for Brummel, who sounds horridly affected," Ellen said, "but what a lovely set-down and, from all I've heard about the Regent's embonpoint, richly deserved."

"Mama met the Prince at Brighton. I remember her telling Papa that he was ever so handsome," Sara told her.

"Handsome is as handsome does, and that was years ago," Ellen snapped.

"La, one would imagine you had a special grudge against him," Sara drawled.

Ellen flushed. "Nothing of the kind." She looked down at Tiffany. "But why do we linger here? I am sure that this child is weary, having traveled so far. You'll want to rest, will you not? I've had a chamber prepared for you."

The thought of her own room was most appealing and she was tired but she would not admit to such a weakness in front of Sara, whom she was disliking more each minute. "Cousin Peter's promised to show me the abbey."

Sara paled. "The . . . the abbey? Why would you promise such a thing, Peter, when you know . . ."

He gave her a half-laughing, half-exasperated look. "I know nothing of the sort."

"But I . . . I tell you, I've heard *chanting.*" She shivered.

" 'Twas the wind in the trees," Ellen said, smiling. "I have lived here nearly all the days of my life and I've yet to hear it. You are fanciful, dearest. I have often told you so."

"It was not the wind!" Sara frowned. "And the servants say that cowled figures have been seen walking there . . ."

"Sara, love, why will you give credence to these silly tales?" Peter frowned.

"They're not silly," she cried. "I—I'd not go near there on the night of the full moon for anything in this world—nor would anyone in the village. It . . . it's a cursed spot." She fastened her eyes on Tiffany. "I tell you, child, if you are wise, you'll stay away from it."

The idea of ghosts was not a pleasant one but Tiffany, lifting her chin, said defiantly, "I should like to go this very moment."

Peter laughed. "Bravo! I commend you for your good sense. But have patience, my dear. I am older than you, and I must confess that I do need to rest before braving the ghostly abbot and his crew of phantom monks." His eyes lingered on Sara's face.

"And I hope you will want to talk to me." Sara's glance was provocative. "You must tell me more about London . . . and did you bring me a surprise—as you promised?"

"As I promised, I did."

"Ah!" She clapped her hands together like a pleased child. "What is it?"

"A surprise," he said, winking.

"Show it to me, then. At once!" she commanded.

"It's in my portmanteau."

"Then, let's find it. I expect Bart's taken it inside." With a little skip, she pushed him toward the door. "Come."

Cocking a laughing eye at his mother, Peter said, "I hear and must obey."

"Of course you must, my love." Ellen smiled. She was silent a moment, watching them as they went inside. Then, turning back to Tiffany, her eyes widened. "Why, child, what's amiss? Why are you crying? Are you homesick already?"

Tiffany could only shake her head. She could not tell this gentle lady that her tears had arisen out of an unexplainable dislike for Sara Wingfield. Nor could she explain the pain that had assailed her as she had seen the way Peter had looked at the girl. "Yes, I . . . I do miss Mama."

Her kindly hostess knelt before her, gathering her to her ample bosom.

"Taffy is a Welshman, Taffy is a thief . . ."

Tom's voice, hideously amplified, boomed in Tiffany's ears. Kneeling in that dark, dank little cell, she screamed loudly, "Come back, Tom. Tom, do not leave me here . . . come back, come back, come ba-a-a-a-aack. Please! Ple-e-e-e-ease!"

But he would not, not ever again, and she would never be found because no one knew where she was. No one knew that the tiny room existed, no one save Tom, who had run away, leaving her alone! "Tom, please come back!" she wailed again.

Something clutched at her, and she screamed again.

"Love, wake up! Wake up."

The voice came from a great distance away. She could scarcely hear it, but there was a hand on her shoulder—the hand of the monster in the darkness, the monster who dwelt in the depths of the cellar! She gasped and struggled.

"Child," —the voice was louder and closer—"wake up!" She was shaken gently and she blinked against the moonlight, knowing that she had been keeping her eyes squeezed shut. The shards of the dream were falling away and she no longer struggled against the gentle pressure on her shoulder.

"There. Do you feel better, my dear?"

It was her Cousin Peter—Peter whose face was outlined in the moonlight and who had little moons reflected in both his eyes. "Oh," she breathed. "I dreamed I was still down there . . . in the cellar." A tremor shook her slight body. To mention the place was to bring its menace close once more.

"The cellar? What cellar, my dear? Tell me about it." He sat on the edge of the bed and his comforting arm was still around her.

She had thought she could never tell anyone about it. Tom had warned her that something terrible would befall her if she did—but Tom was leagues and leagues away and she was safe. "You promise you'll not tell Tom."

"I promise," he whispered. "I shall never tell anyone."

She huddled against him. "It . . . it is in Mrs. Bowes's lodging house—but she does not know about it. It is a cellar beneath a cellar. There's a little door and afterwards steps, many steps. I thought we should never stop going down them."

"Why did you go?"

"Tom said he could hide me."

"Hide you? Why did you want to hide?"

"Oh!" she gasped. "I . . . I told him I was going away and that I did not want to leave Mama. I—I pray you'll not be angry with me."

He stroked her hair gently. "I'm not angry. It is understandable. And you'll see her soon again. Do not fret."

"I shan't. I—I am glad to be here with you. I was just being silly," she murmured ashamedly.

"No, you were not, but never mind that. Tom took you to this cellar, and then what happened?"

"He . . . left me alone in the dark." She shuddered. "He had brought a candle, but he went back up the stairs and at the top, he blew it out and said he'd come back to fetch me after you'd gone. But you were not coming for two days. I thought he was only teasing me, but he went

33

away and it was so dark and cold and I tried to follow him up the stairs but I could not see them and I heard squeaking. There were rats and I was afraid to move."

"Damn and blast him!" Peter muttered. "How long did he leave you there?"

"A long, long time."

"And you did not call out?"

"I did, but no one came. Finally, he returned and he . . . he said I must not tell anyone about what he had done, or some night when I was sleeping, he would come and knock me on the head and drag me down there and never come back for me."

"But your mother must have missed you!"

"She and my stepfather had gone out."

"Well," he said soothingly, "you must know that he could not do as he threatened. And you must not be frightened, either. You are safe here." He gave her a loving little squeeze.

"Oh, I know that," she breathed.

"I do not think you'll have the dream a second time, but should you like a night-light?"

"No," she said disdainfully now. "I am not a baby. I am turned twelve."

"That is a fine age," he agreed solemnly.

"I do not believe that it is—not anymore."

"Do you not? Why not?" Laughter edged his tone.

"I should like to be older."

"You will be one day and will wish to be younger."

"I shan't."

"Why are you so eager to put spurs to time?"

"Because . . ."

"Because why?"

"I . . . I cannot tell you."

"As you choose, child, and . . ." He paused as the clock on the mantelpiece tinged softly. "It grows late, 'tis half past the hour of eleven. Do you think you can sleep now, Tiffany?"

"Yes, if . . ."

"If?"

34

"If you will kiss me good night as . . . as Mama does."

"I shall be honored." His arm tightened about her, and he brushed her cheek with his lips. His hand was in her hair again, stroking it back. "Sweetest dreams, my dear," he said softly, and rising from the bed, he went out of the room.

Tiffany put a hand to her cheek and then held it to her mouth. "Oh," she whispered longingly. "If I were to pray to God, would he make me older faster?" But she knew that he would not, for since her family had moved from the vicinity of St. James Church, they did not attend services anywhere—not having pence to spare for the collection. Under the circumstances, God would have turned his face away from the whole family and it was in vain that she said, "If only I were that Sara's age." She stared through the window at the moon, and the clock had chimed twelve before she finally slept.

Three

Tiffany awakened with the first rays of the sun, and sitting up in bed, she clasped her knees and rested her chin on them. She was thinking about Peter. Putting her hand to her cheek, she pressed it against her mouth and smiled wryly. It was astounding how well she remembered the caress she had shamelessly begged from him that first night at the abbey. She recalled the dream as well—the nightmare that had brought him into her chamber. He had been passing in the hall and heard her screaming— the door had been left ajar by the maidservant who had put her to bed. She could bless the girl for that— unknowingly, she had provided her with a memory that she had cherished through five years of extraordinary changes; five years in which she had achieved at least one childish wish—she had become older. She had, in fact, passed her seventeenth birthday in March, which made her six months into her eighteenth year. But so many other wishes had remained unfulfilled. Inadvertently, that had been her fault. Who would have thought that a twelve-year-old child could have wrought such extraordinary changes upon three lives—five, if she were to be absolutely accurate and include those which no longer counted.

This was a morning for memories. Others were coming fast upon the first and happiest of them. For once she did not close her mind to them; she must bear the pain. In view of what would take place that afternoon, she must examine them. In a sense, it would not be difficult—so much had happened in rapid succession.

"The second morning," she murmured and instantly contradicted herself. It had been her *first* morning at the abbey, though it was hard to recall a time when the mansion had been still a puzzle to her; when every nook and cranny was not yet as familiar as Mrs. Bowes's three noisome rooms had been to the child Tiffany. Yet, she could see that little girl rising early in the morning.

She had darted to the window, delighting in the fact that it overlooked part of the gardens. She had stared excitedly at patterned flower beds and at old stone steps running down a sloping lawn. They were flanked by pillars bearing aged urns filled with trailing vines. The steps ended at a round pool covered with lily pads, and in the center was a pair of mermen holding conch shells from which flowed streams of water. Beyond the fountain was an expanse of clipped grass; beyond that loomed the wooded park. Among its trees lay the ruined abbey. She had not known it was there, had not known she would find it that very morning. Peter had promised to show it to her, but she had discovered it accidently. If she had waited for him to come with her, would she be here now? Would he? It was futile to think of that. There could be no changing those events; they were the past.

In the last five years, Sir Matthew, waxing fortunate at the gaming tables, had won an estate in Ireland, whence he had gone with herself, Mama, and Tom. In the larger world, Napoleon had been defeated and exiled to Elba. He had returned for a hundred terrifying days but after Waterloo, he was languishing on St. Helena. There had been a minor but similar upheaval in the world of fashion. Beau Brummel, hounded by creditors and deprived of princely favor, was exiled to Calais. More recently, the poor Princess Charlotte, heir to the throne of England, had died in childbirth—how Cousin Ellen had wept at that, but everyone had been affected and it was said that the Prince had not yet recovered his spirits. However, there was no doubt but that Cousin Ellen had grown very emotional since Peter . . . She drew a pained breath—she would not think about that. Her memories must be orderly—go back, back, back to that first morning and herself still at the window, seeing Sara, dressed for riding, run down the steps. She had assumed that the stables lay in that direction. Odd how she had disliked Sara, had even made a face at her, as she moved out of sight. Of course, she had been jealous—a snatch of conversation from the night of her arrival came back to her.

Sara was seated at the dining table, her hand straying to a necklace of carved carnelians set in gold. "See? It is nearly the color of my hair. Oh, Peter, it is lovely."

"Soon I shall give you diamonds and emeralds, my own dearest." He had been so very much in love with Sara Wingfield and unable to conceal it, quite unable to keep from looking at her as if she were a goddess on a pedestal.

There was music in Tiffany's ears—sounds remained in her mind just as sights did. She had heard it issuing from the chamber that she now knew was the music room; it was to the left of the stairs on the ground floor. Passing it, she had been beguiled by those wonderful sounds—sweet, sad, wailing. Entranced, she had paused to listen. There had been fiddlers on London's streets— but what a difference. This music filled her with sorrow one moment, and the next she had wanted to dance. She had dared to open the door a crack, and found that it was Peter who was playing. She remembered that she had heard the sound of a violin that afternoon she and her mother had come to see him.

A tap on her shoulder startled her. She turned to find Mrs. Greene, the housekeeper, at her side.

"The master'll not like bein' interrupted," she had

whispered. " 'E'll be in a fair fury if 'e sees you; best come away, child."

She had obeyed. But she had been unable to believe that the man who had come to her chamber the previous night, the man with whom she had traveled for four days, could ever be in a fury. Furies were for Sir Matthew. How little she had known about Peter in those days—but she was getting ahead of herself again. She must return to that younger Tiffany, follow her image as if she were in a playhouse; watching the child she had been, on the stage of her mind.

Still half-enthralled by the music, she had wandered down the corridor and through an open door which brought her into the very part of the garden she had seen from her window.

"If I had not gone . . . if I had come out of another door . . ." she whispered sadly.

But she had come out into the gardens near the stone steps with their guardian pillars and urns. She had run down the steps to sit on the rim of the fountain and gaze into the water. She had glimpsed goldfish among the lily pads, and she had seen the reflection of the sky and of the trees and above them a shattered stone facade centered by the rusty iron frame of a rose window. Excitement had thrilled through her—an excitement tinged with awe and perhaps fear. She had seen similar windows in churches—she must have found the abbey—the haunted abbey!

Turning toward the trees, she had looked for it, not seeing those broken stones at first, but she had caught a yellow glint through the leaves. Anticipation had vanquished her fears and she had run through grass still wet with morning dew. Skirting the trees, she had found the huge stumps of pillars, the broken walls, and the flat slabs of cross-carved gravestones with their worn Latin inscriptions. Did the abbey's ghostly monks arise from these buried sepulchers? She quailed—but she must not be cowardly. Peter would scoff. Yet, she wished she had waited for him, wished that he walked at her side and held her hand. Then, she had stopped, frozen into immobility as she had heard the laughter—light, eerie, disembodied in that place of shattered stones. A scream swelled in her throat emerging as soundless as a breath. If only she had given some indication of her presence—but she had not and, unaware that any save the girl in his arms could hear, the man continued bitterly, "Why are you laughing?"

"I told you why."

Tiffany threw a hand across her mouth stifling yet another cry. "But damn the brat, she may come here yet, for all my tales of ghosts. We'll need to find another place. We must be cautious."

"We 'ave been cautious." The man laughed again. "Ye'll drop no bastard on the Jew's sheets, Sara."

"Enough, you know I do not like such talk."

"Do ye not? Per'aps, I'd better go, my fine lady."

"Not yet. Hold me, Tim."

There was a silence before he groaned. "Damn ye for a witch. God, a man could drown in your green eyes."

"Oh, my love, my Tim," she panted.

"God, to think of ye wi' the Jew."

"Think of his gold, instead."

"Damn 'is gold. Come away wi' me, Sara."

"And sleep in ditches, love? Better for you to stay."

"I'll not 'ave the crumbs from 'is table."

"He'll have the crumbs and you the feast, that I swear. But I must go now."

"So soon?"

"It's safer thus. Tomorrow the moon'll be full and when it rises, I'll meet you here and none to disturb us for fear of ghosts, the fools. We'll have the whole night."

"Ye promise."

"On my life—come moonrise. That is, if you've no fear of the monks."

"If they were twenty devils, I'd come to ye."

The images in Tiffany's mind wavered like moonlight on a rock-struck pool. She did not want to see Sara creep out from the large crevice in the adjacent wall, her hair tangled and her lips fuller, redder, as if swollen by her lover's kisses. She did not want to see a man in rough work clothes follow her—but inevitably, his image arose—his heavy, but handsome features, his hair ripely yellow, his blue eyes warm as he exchanged a look with Sara and hastily disappeared among the trees while she, carefully buttoning her collar, strode off in another direction.

Little Tiffany, crouched in the foliage, had been torn between indignation and pain. There had been other feelings which had given her odd bodily pangs which, even now, she did not fully understand. Uppermost in her mind, however, was the knowledge that Peter was being cheated by this girl to whom he had given his heart—cheated and mocked.

In spite of that, she did not want to remember the subsequent events, but there was no halting the progression of those images. She saw herself sobbing, then resolutely wiping her tears away. In that moment, she had made the decision which had brought about the upheaval. If only she might have foreseen what would happen! At twelve, however, she had been concerned only with the present. In the present, Sara's perfidy must be exposed. How?

She might have told Peter what she had overheard, but having lived for three years in Sir Matthew's household, she knew she would not be believed. Sara would deny everything and denounce her as a liar as Tom had done once when she had revealed his stealing from her mother's reticule. It was she who had been punished, not he. Yet, Peter must be alerted!

"Oh, God," Tiffany whispered, falling back on her pillows. "But I could not have known . . ."

Thought accelerated time. It was the following day. Impossible to fill those succeeding hours with any cohesive imagery; she did not remember anything about her second day at Clive Abbey. She could only recall that the skies had been clear and that late in the afternoon, she had heard Sara say with a pronounced shiver, " 'Twill be a full moon tonight."

Peter had laughed and teased her. She had responded with unwonted sharpness, then turned soft and fond. Seeing his adoring glances, Tiffany had been strengthened in her resolve. By then, she had determined a course of action. It had pleased her and she had actually prayed that nothing go wrong with Sara's plans. That evening, she had waited on tenterhooks for Sara's announcement that she had the headache. It had not come—but her place at table was empty, and Cousin Ellen had explained that she had turned feverish.

Peter had shaken his head. "The full moon," he had sighed.

It had been warm that night and they had sat in the garden watching the sunset. The sound of frogs and crickets had been loud in her ears and occasionally she had been startled by the hoot of an owl flying overhead on silent wings.

"Should not Tiffany be put to bed?"

Tiffany started, gazing nervously about her sunlit bedchamber; the voice in her head had sounded amazingly real, but, of course, it had issued from Cousin Ellen's lips as she had sat beside Peter in the darkening garden.

"Please, not yet, I do not want to go to bed yet," the little girl begged.

If Cousin Ellen had insisted—but it was never in her nature to insist.

Peter had been preoccupied. If he had not spoken at that moment—but he did, half-ruefully, half-amusedly. "It's a fine night. Let the child enjoy it. At least she's not intimidated by ghostly monks and cowering in her chamber."

His mother had smiled tolerantly. "Sara's still at an age when such terrors are mighty appealing, and she's devoted to the works of Mrs. Radcliffe."

Be still. Say nothing, Tiffany begged her image but inexorably, the child she had been said, "I'd never be afraid of ghosts." She could also remember her feelings of triumph as she uttered this sentiment. Here had been the opening she had craved, and it had not even been of her creating! She had continued in a wheedling tone, "I pray you, Cousin Peter, will you not show me the abbey ruins?"

43

"You wish to see them *now?*" he had asked incredulously.

"Yes, please."

He shook his head, " 'Twould only give you bad dreams."

"I should not be afraid if you were with me."

"Now here's bravery," he smiled. "I wish my Sara shared your gumption, but—I think not, dear."

She had jumped up. "Please. I am not afraid."

"If Sara were here, you'd shame her from her terrors."

"You may tell her you showed *me* the abbey in the dark and I was not afraid." She had been persistent, begging, teasing, cajoling until he had regarded her oddly.

"Why are you so determined upon this adventure, Tiffany?"

Unwittingly, Cousin Ellen had aided her. "She's a romantic like her mother. Mary used to love to go strolling in the moonlight. Why don't you take her, Peter?"

"Very well, but you must not blame me if nightmares gallop across your pillow this night."

"They'll not," she had said confidently, unaware of all the tortured dreams and agonizing regrets the excursion would spawn.

It was dark when they went down the garden stairs. The full moon, small and white, hung over the trees and was reflected in the fountain. "If I'd not started immediately for the woods, would he have guessed?"

There was no answering that query. She had run ahead in the direction she had taken the first time. He, following, had said with some amusement, "I believe you've been to the abbey already."

"No." She had danced back to him across the lawn.

"You seem to know its direction."

"Is that the direction?"

"It lies in those woods."

"Oh."

If they had had more to say to each other as they had moved across the grass, would Sara and her lover have been alerted? Why had they not spoken? Because, she believed, both of them had been mesmerized by the beauty about them—by the silvered treetops, by the hush in the air, by the dark blue of a sky massed with stars and finally by the broken stones of the abbey, massive and mysterious in the moonlight.

Her heart had climbed to her throat. Had they arrived too early, had her ruse been for naught? It was so quiet—too quiet. Her sense of direction had been excellent. Unfalteringly, she had made her way around the trees, nearing the spot where she had heard their voices on the previous morning. Her image approached the shattered wall, nearing the crevice through which Sara had crawled. She had cast a glance over her shoulder. Peter was just behind her. The moonlight showed her his face, eyes narrowed.

Run away, run, run, run, Tiffany begged her image. He knows you've been there before, he does not know your purpose in bringing him there! Sara do not laugh!

Inevitably it came, the laughter—rich, earthy, wanton, rising from that space behind the wall, echoing down the years, the only real specter that haunted the abbey.

Peter had halted.

Do not speak, Sara!

"Damn and blast you, Tim, you've torn my gown!"

"Take it off, then. 'Ere, I'll 'elp you, love."

"I'll catch my death," she giggled.

"I'll warm ye, love."

Peter might have been one of the stone columns, he stood so still.

You stay still too, Tiffany begged that triumphant image.

She had not stayed still. She had seized his hand, pulling him toward the crevice in the wall. He had wrenched his hand away and strode to the wall, and she in hot pursuit had accompanied him, crawling up on the broken stones, staring down as he stared down at Sara topped by Tim.

"There!" Tiffany had cried.

"Sara!"

Would she ever forget the agony in Peter's voice? Would she ever forget the vindictive look that Sara had given her when— But she was getting ahead of herself. First there was the shrill scream as Sara, hair tumbled, gown gaping open on her full bosom, arose to stare unbelievingly up at Peter. Her eyes moved to Tiffany's face and then that look! Behind her, mouth agape, was Sara's lover, naked to the waist. An instant later, he had vaulted the wall, and pushed Peter down. Then, he jumped back, and seizing the gasping, sobbing Sara by the hand, had fled into the woods.

Tiffany had knelt by the fallen man. "Are you hurt?" she had cried.

His eyes, dazed at first, had fastened on her face. Then, as before, they had narrowed. "You knew!" Catching her arm in a hurtful grip, he had sat up, saying harshly, "Tell me the truth. You *knew*."

"Yes, I . . . h-heard them making plans to meet here. They were here yesterday morning too." She had faltered, wondering at anger that seemed directed at her. "I thought you ought to know."

"Did you?" he had said in a low voice. "Did you, you misbegotten little sneak! Damn you!" he had snarled. "Get away from me. I do not want to look at you."

She had fled into the woods and fallen heavily. He, following, had grabbed her up and carried her back to the house and up to her chamber, where having wept until her tears had dried up, she fell into an exhausted slumber.

The next morning, he had passed her in the hall, his face stony, his eyes chill. He had seemed not to see her.

"Cousin Peter," she had whispered.

He had not responded.

"I—I thought you must know!" she had cried desperately.

"Yes, I expect I had to know," he had answered finally. "Am I to thank you for that?" He had strode away from her quickly, as if he could not bear to look at her. From the maid who tended her, she heard he had sent men to search for Sara—but she and her lover might have vanished into thin air.

She had expected Cousin Ellen would send her home, for she had gone to her and sobbingly explained what she had done. But much to her surprise, she had been told, "I have no blame for you." Ellen Medina's gaze had strayed into the distance. "I am the one who must be blamed." She had added distractedly, "Run away and play, my child."

Tiffany had not understood her words. The explanation had come a fortnight later when Cousin Ellen, looking pale and distraught, had told her that Peter had gone. "He'll not be back," she had sighed.

"It . . . it's all my fault," Tiffany had wailed.

"No, the blame is mine," her cousin had repeated. "Sara was a pretty child and well-connected. My reasons for bringing her here were not entirely unselfish. I cherished a hope that when they were older, they might come to love each other. Peter had always had a fondness for her. I encouraged it. I encouraged them both. I told Peter that Sara loved him, and told Sara that Peter adored her.

"I knew her to be a trifle acquisitive, I begged him to buy her little presents. He was nineteen; of course, he was fond of her—but not overly interested in a thirteen-year-old girl. Besides, there was his music. But as she grew older, I could see he was beginning to find her very beguiling. I continued to nurture this particular bud, and finally, last year, he told me that he did love her, and she shyly confessed that she had come to love him.

"I had qualms about it. It seemed to me that she was too glib in her protestations, but I blinded myself on purpose. I knew that if he married, he would settle down and stay here. Peter, you see, was torn—he loved his music.

"He was a mere infant when his father put a violin into his hands. He loved it then. When he was scarcely three, he was already playing little pieces; his father said he had a gift. I knew that gift would take him away from

47

me. I . . . I came between my dear husband and his music—he should have been free, but because we fell in love and ran away together, he had to continue tutoring. We were very happy—ecstatically happy, the three of us. But I know that Esdras yet regretted the career he might have had, were he not encumbered with a family. You see, you do not *have* musical talent—it has *you*. It rules you, it comes between you and all that you love. It can raise you to the heights and drop you to the depths.

"I did not want this existence for Peter, but I can see now that I should not have interfered. I am, I think, glad that he is doing as he wished to do." And she had wept.

The grieving child had derived little comfort from that guilt-ridden confession. It did not assuage her own feelings of guilt and regret. Furthermore, she had not entirely understood what Ellen had been saying. She understood it now—now that the name of Simon Esdras, the name Peter had taken, emblazoned on handbills and posters, was known from Vienna to St. Petersburg, from Moscow to New York.

Simon Esdras was as famous a virtuoso as his friend Paganini. Concerti were written for Esdras—kings and queens ordered that he play for them. In the music room, a glass case held decorations awarded to him by the Austrian emperor, President Madison, and a host of German princes. He had played before Louis XVIII of France and for the King of Sweden. He had spent the winter of 1817 touring Russia. Consequently, she should have no fear in seeing him again. If it had not been for her intervention, he would have wed his wanton Sara and remained in the obscurity of his Yorkshire estate. Yet, she was nervous, for she had not seen him in all the five years that had passed since his departure.

His visits to his mother had been rare and hurried. Tiffany had been in Dublin when he had first come home. When Sir Matthew had lost the estate on another turn of the cards, Tiffany had gone back to Cousin Ellen—but Peter had been in Vienna. Other visits had taken place when she was in Edinburgh where Sir Matthew was battening on the generosity of a distant cousin. Then, there had been Tom's disgrace. Caught poaching, he had been sentenced to two years in prison. It was a lighter punishment than usual; he could have been transported. But the presiding judge, impressed by his family background, threw the blame for his failings on the men with whom he had been arrested. However, though he must have been released by now, Lady Mary had had no word of him. That was not unexpected, for Sir Matthew, losing heavily at the gaming tables, had shot himself, leaving his wife and stepdaughter penniless. Of course, Cousin Ellen had sent for them, but only Tiffany had come. Lady Mary had been invited to stay with her Cousin Anne, who had inherited a house and still resided in Edinburgh. Now, astonishingly, Lady Mary was wed again to Lord Cavendish, a wealthy widower who had come to Scotland for the shooting. They had met at a dance in Edinburgh's Assembly Rooms.

They had gone on a honeymoon to Italy and would, Lady Mary had written, return in late August—at which time Tiffany would join them. She had anticipated their return earlier this week and she wished they had already arrived, for Peter, who had concluded a round of concerts in Austria, was on his way back to the abbey. He had been expected the previous day but there had been a bad rainstorm, and, no doubt, he was stranded somewhere on the mired roads.

Slipping out of bed, Tiffany took a nervous turn around her chamber. Moving to the window, she scanned the sky. A cloud had blotted out the sun and other clouds were appearing. It was possible that there would be more rain. She would not be sorry for that—not if it hindered Peter's arrival. She shook her head. She was being utterly selfish. Cousin Ellen lived for his visits! She had been preparing for his homecoming all that week, and the cook had been busy making his favorite pasties. Furthermore, it was time that she forgot her fears at meeting him again. She must continue to remind herself that she *had,* however er inadvertently, helped him to realize his ambitions and saved him from an unfortunate marriage.

Yet, in spite of his present celebrity, would not the sight of her cause him to remember that terrible night? In five years, she had learned something about masculine pride. Would not the fact that she had been a witness to Sara's cruel betrayal stand between them? Would it not keep them from being friends ever again? She could not restrain a little moan. She did not want to be his friend. There was a far deeper reason behind the anxiety with which she viewed their pending reunion. Though she had changed from child to woman, one factor had not changed. At twelve, she had fallen in love with Peter Medina, and though she was nearly eighteen, she still loved him. Furthermore, she was dismally sure that she would love him all the rest of her days.

Four

"Rain." There was disappointment in Ellen Medina's tone as she stood at the window of the music room, looking up at the rolling, leaking clouds.

Tiffany, leaning against the old rosewood pianoforte, cast an eye at the clock. Its hands pointed to four. She felt vaguely guilty, as though her half-wish had been granted. She felt it incumbent upon her to say soothingly, "The day's not at an end yet, Cousin Ellen."

"It's no weather to brave our roads," Ellen mourned, running a nervous hand through her graying hair.

Feeling more guilty than ever, Tiffany moved to the glass-enclosed table containing some of Peter's decorations, neatly mounted on dark blue velvet. Gazing down, she met her own reflection and smiled wryly at it, trying to imagine what he would think when he saw her. Even if he did not come that day or the next, ultimately they would meet. She had changed. In one brief summer—her thirteenth—she had gained two inches. A year later, an-

other one had been added. She had been disappointe
that no more had come, but Lady Mary had bee
pleased. "Men feel protective of little women," she ha
stated.

Tiffany had refrained from mentioning that Sir Ma
thew was hardly protective. She wondered about h
mother's new husband, Garnet Bland, Lord Cavendisl
She had not met him as yet.

Ellen had been delighted. "Your poor mother neec
some romance in her life."

That remark had set Tiffany wondering about he
father, whom Lady Mary never discussed, except to mer
tion his military status—he had been a captain—and the
he had been killed in action in his native Ireland. Tiffar
shook her head. Her mind was wandering far afield—a
usual, she was trying not to think of Peter. Yet, converse
ly, she wished him already with them and the ordeal ove
Physically, if not mentally, she was prepared for him. TI
glass told her that she looked very good. Her gown,
blue lutestring, was not new, but the color became he
She had only two good dresses, though her mother ha
written from Italy describing lengths of Florentine si
which had been purchased especially for Tiffany ar
which would be given to Madame Le Gros, one of tl
most fashionable London mantua makers.

Thinking of that letter, she smiled. Between descrij
tions of her new happiness, the new Lady Cavendi
made glowing promises concerning Tiffany's London se
son and the ball which would launch it.

"I vow you'll have a new gown for every hour in tl
day. I do love the fashions. I have given a Roman mantu
maker your measurements and thus will be able to brii
you a new gown when we return. It will have the late
body, which is fuller than before. I am glad of that. I a
assured that we will never go back to the days whe
females dampened their gowns so as to appear near
unclad! Indeed, Signora Grimaldi, the mantua maker
have mentioned—and who is regarded as the finest
Italy—tells me that before many years are out, we sha
go garbed in the full skirts of our grandmother's day.

am not sure I care for that prophecy, for I think it well to show the shape if one is fortunate enough to possess one. The ladies of Rome are very elegant but plump. I have told Garnet that I find them quite beautiful but he insists he cannot abide flashing eyes and black hair. He says he is convinced that I am the most beautiful woman he has ever seen! I have told him, however, that he has yet to meet my daughter. When he does, I know that I shall be quite cast into the shade."

Tiffany laughed, thinking that even though her mother had reached the great age of thirty-five, no one was likely to cast any shade upon her. In spite of the miseries of her late marriage, she had lost nothing in looks. Tiffany examined herself in the glass and decided that if there were any shade to be cast, it must fall upon her. Though there was still a resemblance between her and her mother, she lacked Lady Mary's porcelain delicacy—her eyes were larger, her mouth fuller, her cheekbones higher, and her hair a more ruddy gold. Her eyes wandered down to her gown again and she smoothed it, wishing she were wearing one of the promised silks. The blue lutestring was fine enough but it was not stylish, and Peter, playing before the crowned heads of Europe, must certainly see the most beautiful and fashionable females. Suddenly she laughed!

She was really foolish. In contemplating the past, she had given no thought to the present. Ceasing to regard her own reflection, she examined Peter's decorations—the enameled crosses centered with rubies, diamonds or emeralds. The gold violin with the diamond bow affixed to it, the emerald star and others equally magnificent. Each of these pieces represented a concert or a series of concerts. An echo of applause was in her ears—there would have been cheering, too, and his name shouted to the rafters. She had been thinking of the unhappy young man who had gone forth from his house five years ago. But he was no longer that young man—he was Simon Esdras, the great, the widely acclaimed virtuoso!

A draught of cold air fanned her cheek. Behind her, Ellen cried, "My love!"

Turning swiftly, Tiffany found that a tall dark man in a rain-spattered, many-caped coat had stepped across the threshold of the music room. He was wearing a high silk hat, and one slim hand rested on a silver-topped ebony cane. He dropped the cane to take his mother in his arms. Releasing her, he looked in Tiffany's direction.

She took a step forward. His name sprang to her lips, and then she closed them without uttering the word. Meeting his curious but uninterested glance, she realized that all her fears had been for naught. It was only too obvious that he had not the least idea who she was.

With the coming of night, the rain had stopped, and the skies were, for the most part, dark blue with only patches of white clouds remaining. A half-moon was caught in the second branch of an elm tree. At least, so it looked from where Tiffany stood. She had come from the music room, whence she and Cousin Ellen had retired after dinner, leaving Peter to his port.

Now, unmindful of the damp, moisture-laden wind, she stood surveying the curve of the driveway. She wished she were nearing the end of it, passing the stone gatehouse, going in the direction of the road. If only she had relatives in London, she might have gone to them. She would rather be anywhere than under a roof that sheltered both herself and Peter Medina. The thought of the meals she must take with him sitting at the head of the table sent a shiver through her. The thought of inadvertently meeting him in the halls or outside on the grounds brought forth another shiver. She, who had been so wracked with unhappy memories that morning, found these obliterated by the events of the last few hours.

It had begun with Cousin Ellen's surprised, tentative, "Peter, my dear, you remember your Cousin Tiffany, do you not?"

There had been a slight frown in his eyes. Then, it had vanished as he had nodded, giving her an impersonal smile. "Cousin Tiffany." His tone had grown a little warmer as he had continued, "You must excuse me, my dear. I did not recognize you. You have grown. Indeed, you are quite the young lady."

She gritted her teeth. She would, she realized, have preferred that he had snarled or raged or cut her dead—anything rather than questioning her with such disinterested politeness about her family. She had been only too right—he was certainly not that unhappy and vulnerable youth who had gone forth from this house half a decade ago. He was a world-famous violinist who had drunk deep from the well of success. And she hated him!

Strolling into the music room, Peter smiled at his mother, "Where's our little cousin? Gone to bed so soon?"

Ellen regarded him a moment before answering. "I expect she has. You did not remember her?" There was a faint thread of accusation in her tone.

He paused and then said coldly, "I remembered her. Five years have not changed her to that extent. Besides I had your letter telling me she was here. When will her mother send for her?"

She frowned. "Whenever she returns from the continent. It should be soon." She added, "Why were you so unkind to the child?"

"Did you think me unkind?"

"You spoke to her as if she were a stranger."

"It is how I regard her."

Ellen hesitated. In five years she had not mentioned Sara Wingfield or the circumstances attendant upon her disappearance. Still, she was sure Peter had dismissed her from his mind. Though she knew little of his life on the concert circuit, she had traveled enough with his father to know that performing artists were seldom celibate. Young, handsome men such as her son had their pick of women—highborn beauties besieged their dressing rooms or followed them from the halls. And their art itself was a powerful stimulant to passion—the two seemed intertwined. She bit down a sigh. That was another reason she had not wanted that wild uncertain life for her son—but it was his. Consequently she could not keep a shade of incredulity from her voice as she asked, "You cannot sti think on Sara?"

"Sara?" A derisive smile played about his mouth "No."

"Yet in some way you've bracketed Sara and Tiffan together, even though I told you at the time, the chil meant no harm. Why do you resent her?"

"You are mistaken, Mother. I resent neither them. Each, in her own way, taught me some vital truth about her sex. I cannot resent that."

"And what did Tiffany teach you?"

"About feminine duplicity—or trickery, if you like."

"Because it was she who revealed Sara's perfidy?"

"Because of the sly way she revealed it. If she' given me some warning, some hint . . ."

"Would you have believed her warnings or h hints? You were besotted by Sara. The child knew it. Sl chose the only way she could. She wanted you to see. know that for a fact. I know, too, that it broke her hea when you turned on her."

"Broke her heart?" he repeated caustically. "A twelve?"

"Oh, Peter, I wish you knew her better."

"I might say the same of you, Mama."

Ellen raised troubled eyes. "Tiffany loved you, P ter. And I have the feeling she loves you still."

"*Tant pis.*" He shrugged. "The love of women—"

"Can be constant and should not be dismissed lightly—from wherever it comes," she said tartly. "I fe you are spoiled, my son."

"Forearmed. I love but one woman and she's stan ing, or rather sitting, before me." He smiled at Ellen. "A for the rest . . ."

"In five years, you've found no one to replace Sara?"

"On the contrary, I have found many. They flutt about me like bright moths, ready to be burned in t flames. I am always obliging with a candle, Mama—b not with love. It's difficult to believe in an emotion whi can be so easily assumed. A downcast eye, a heavi bosom, a tremulous smile, a sigh, a kiss or two or three . . ."

"Pray do not continue. You are too easily disillusioned. We are not all like Sara."

"I've said that you are not, Mama." Stooping, he bore her hand to his lips and kissed it. Releasing it with a loving little squeeze, he added, "Now I think I need some fresh air. I pray you will excuse me for the nonce. I shan't be long."

"Of course, my dear." Watching him go, Ellen felt close to tears. Amongst them, two well-intentioned females—and a third who was less well-meaning—had insulated him against all commitment; and, of the three, she still held herself the most to blame. She had tried to control his destiny and Sara's too. She had been wrong, she had deserved to fail. But they had not deserved what had happened to them. If there were only some way to right that wrong, but that too was beyond her control.

Peter, striding down the hall, felt restless. As usual, he was of two minds. He enjoyed coming home—he had always loved the abbey. But once he was there, the memory of Sara lolling in the arms of her stableboy, arose to taunt him. Though he had long ceased to love her, the bitterness remained. She had been so clever—her little touches, her kisses, shy but with just a hint of budding passion in them. Her ardent looks, all feigned! And the child Tiffany to whom he had felt so drawn was another Sara in embryo. Never could he forget or forgive her duplicity on the night she had conducted him to the ruins!

No matter what his mother said, the only difference between Tiffany and Sara was age and experience. In another few months, Tiffany would be launched in society. He could only pity those unfortunates who would be drawn into her snare. By this time, she must have grown much more artful. She would never make the mistakes she had made on the night she had enticed him to the abbey. He smiled derisively. She had pretended she did not know the way, but he, following, had soon perceived that she did. She could probably have walked it blind-folded!

Why had she played that cruel trick on him?

His mother had called it "love." His mother must yet be besotted by her charm. Or perhaps she was too intrinsically good to believe the worst of a child. Yet, how could she imagine that any tender passion had motivated Tiffany that night. A twelve-year-old could know nothing of love! To his mind, it was a warped sense of humor. As she had confessed, she had heard Sara make the assigna-tion. As she had not confessed, she had wanted to see the fur fly. That was the only logical way to look at it. Certainly it was a poor return for his effort to remove her from her stepfather's clutches. Why had he done it? He did not need to ask himself that question. He could still remember his shock at the sight of her delicate little face, so badly bruised. It had hurt him. She had seemed such a winning child. His lip curled. Perhaps there was a reason for that punishment? Perhaps rather than being the tyrant he had imagined him to be, Sir Matthew had been a victim and reacted accordingly. He himself had wanted to beat her that night. Yet, in a sense, he should be grateful to her—she had freed him from Sara and opened his eyes to all women!

That was a great boon. The temptations that beset an artist were many. He thought of Nicolo Paganini who had interrupted his career for two years for the love of some Tuscan noblewoman. The episode had taken place sixteen years earlier, but it still caused a fire to sparkle in Paganini's eyes whenever he mentioned Tuscany. And now poor Nicolo had succumbed again and fallen into the toils of La Bianchi, the singer, when his only real mistress should be his muse—the which he had said to him.

"Ah, Simone." Nicolo had smiled. "Of all my loves, is the violin the greatest. But beautiful as is her shape, she is cold in bed."

"If so you believe, you are safe." Peter had also laughed. He could not fault those pleasures Paganini praised. In five years, many women had warmed his bed.

Nearly all of them had slipped between his sheets with words of love. He could not remember any of them. No, that was not quite accurate. He could remember the name of Helena, whom he had left five nights ago. He laughed and let himself out the front door. However, his laughter ceased quickly as he heard a startled gasp and saw Tiffany dash across the grass only to disappear abruptly with a cry of alarm.

He hurried in that direction and saw that she had fallen on the wet grass. She lay there, her shoulders shaking. "Good God, have you hurt yourself then?" He knelt beside her.

"No. I just—fell . . ."

"I see you did and cannot lie there—so. Here, let me help you up. What made you run away? Did I startle you?"

"Oh, Peter." She lifted a face streaked with tears. "There . . . there was no other way to . . . show you and . . . and you had to know. You could not go on believing she loved you. I heard her. It was so cruel! I could not bear for you to be hurt . . . the way Mama was."

"The way your mother was?" he repeated incredulously. "What are you saying, my dear?"

"They quarreled so dreadfully at home. She had thought he loved her but it was only the money, her dowry . . ."

Quite coldly, he said, "I do not see what this can have to do with me. Come—let me take you back to the house."

"You do see." She clutched his hand. "You cannot have forgotten. I loved you . . . love you still. I could not stand by and see you wed to *her*. I'd have told you what I overheard that day, but you'd not have believed me. I told about Tom once and they, like you, called me a sneak . . . and a liar. I did not lie, but they did not want to believe, because he had stolen some of his father's money." She began to tremble. "If you knew what I felt when I heard her with *him*. I—I wanted to *bite* her! You were so good and she—she talked about c-crumbs."

"Crumbs?"

"He said he'd not have the—the crumbs from your table, and she said 'twas you'd have the crumbs and he the f-feast and I—I could not bear it, Peter." Hiding her face in her hands, she began to cry bitterly.

In spite of himself, Peter was moved. There could be no doubt but that she was telling the truth. Hardly knowing what he was doing, he gathered her into his arms. "Tiffany." He held her against him. "Dear, you must not cry."

"I loved you," she sobbed again. "I thought I must die of it when you'd not look at me. For five years, I have wanted to—to tell you so that you'd understand why I led you to them. And—and tonight you looked at me as if I were a stranger, and I—I—I knew you'd never forgive me."

"But I do forgive you, my poor child," he said huskily. "Indeed, I fear it's I who must ask your forgiveness. It was a shock, you see. I—I'd no notion. None." His voice was colored by the old hurt and the old fury. "She was very artful . . ."

"She was wicked!" Tiffany cried. "I hated her. I shall always hate her!"

"She's not worth the spending of so much emotion. She is gone. Do not think on her, poor child."

"Do you—can you really forgive me, Peter?" she asked in a small voice.

"Yes . . . yes, I do. I do understand." As he had done on a night years before, he stroked the tangled hair back from her face, and as he gazed down at her, he experienced a shock. It was as if he were seeing her for the first time, and in a sense, he realized he was. When he had arrived that afternoon, the old smoldering anger had held him yet in thrall. He had greeted her, looked at her—but he had not seen her. Now her hair, moon-gilded, flowed back from a lovely, beguiling face. Was it a trick of that same moonlight that made her tilted eyes so large? He did not believe that. And her mouth was beautiful—the tender curves of childhood yet remained, but it was fuller and dangerously inviting. He felt a stirring of his pulses and his heart was pounding heavily. He could not continue to hold her in his arms; she was not the sad little waif he had borne back to the abbey, five years earlier. He said tentatively, "Child," and paused uncertainly.

It was as though the thought coursing through his mind had leaped into her head. "I am not a child any longer, Peter. Do you not see that?"

"I see it." He tried to sound indulgent. "But you are very young and—"

"I love you, Peter."

There was no doubting her sincerity. It was in her eyes, her voice, and in the yielding softness of her body as she moved against him. He, who had ceased to believe in these protestations, had perforce to believe in her. There was no artifice here, there was only truth; and he made a disquieting discovery. Years ago, he had been drawn to the child. Consequently, her so-called betrayal of his affections had given him a violent shock. Now he knew the truth, and divested of those prejudices in which he had clothed her for the past five years, she had become a danger—a hazard to his peace of mind.

If he held her much longer, he would lose control. "My dearest." He paused. He had not intended to say "dearest." He tried to rectify the error by moving back, but she was still cradled in his arms, and he had not the strength to release her. He stared down at her, deep into her eyes. It was as though they had become magnets, drawing him toward her. He could no longer resist that pull and, for the moment, all thought ceased as their lips met.

He was the first to break away. His pleasure in the embrace was tinctured with guilt. He was not used to refusing the women who offered themselves to him, but this was not one of those teasing, predatory creatures. Tiffany might have turned seventeen, but she was caught in an old dream—one that had tangled him in its snare as well. Now his brain was frantically reasserting its mastery and sending out warning signals. It reminded him that kisses had long ceased to have any meaning beyond the moment. They were a pleasure to be enjoyed when he was not practicing or performing. The feelings—rather, the sensations they aroused did not linger, nor did those who offered them expect that they would. In the morning, he would ease himself from their tumbled couches and hurry to another engagement, another city. No commitments were ever made, not on either side. Why did he fear a commitment had been made now, in this moment which seemed plucked from a long-distant past? Half-fearfully, he drew back, but in looking at her, he was lost again, drowned in a wonderful sweetness. He covered her face with gentle little kisses. Their lips met a second time, and an emotion he once imagined he had felt for Sara Wingfield took hold of him; but now, he realized, he had never known it before. The word "love" took on a newer, deeper, more rapturous meaning. But though it clove to his tongue, wanting to be uttered, he would not obey its prompting—not because he was still unable to believe in it, but because it had opened a door through which he was as yet reluctant to pass.

The post chaise was dark green with the Cavendish coat of arms etched in a deep red on its doors—a bow to the generations of Bland, who rejoiced in the name Garnet. It was drawn by four high-stepping chestnuts, overseen by a coachman in a dark green livery with a maroon collar and two rows of bright gold buttons down his swelling chest. A postboy in similar garb rode one of the horses, and clinging to the back of the equipage was a smart young footman also in green.

Inside sat Lady Mary Cavendish in a blue bombazine dress trimmed with alternating borders of braided crepe and Spanish puffs. Her feet were shod in dark blue chamois sandles, and her slight form swathed in a magnificent cloak of moleskin cloth lined with dark blue sarcenet. She was wearing an absolute treasure of a bonnet, a Paris creation in straw, trimmed in dark blue roses with a brim that shaded her face but did nothing to conceal it from an admiring world. Indeed, until she had fetched her daughter from the abbey, she had been conscious of looking her absolute best.

She knew she had made a very favorable impression on her Cousin Ellen and she had read admiration in Peter Medina's eyes. That was indubitably a feather in her cap for certainly he had seen many beautiful, stylish women in his travels. He himself was a very handsome man and certainly more polished than he had been when he was younger—even if she could not approve his profession. In fact, she had had some hesitancy about explaining it to Garnet, but he had taken it in stride, fully appreciating the difficulties attendant upon being part Jewish in a society as closed as that in England. His censure had been all for Ellen, who never should have given in to her emotions, no matter how attractive the late Esdras Medina had seemed to her.

"In so doing, my dear," he had said, "she closed all doors to herself and to her son. So it cannot matter that he is a violinist."

Though Mary had been tactful enough not to leap to her defense, she could not find it in her heart to heap too much blame upon dear Ellen, who had been so kind to her all those years ago. She flushed as she remembered the full extent of her kindness with never a word of blame. Yet, she was very glad that Garnet had been unable to come with her when she collected Tiffany from the abbey. Though perhaps if he had been there, the girl would not have embarrassed them all by weeping and saying that she wanted to remain with Cousin Ellen.

Her attitude had been most disappointing and embarrassing. It had quite spoiled her pleasure at seeing her daughter again. She wiped a tear from her eye. One would think that after a separation of nearly a year, Tiffany would have been delighted; especially when she discovered that she was going to be driven back to London in such style, stopping at all the best hostelries. Furthermore, her disagreeable daughter had not even been impressed by the fact that Lady Mary had brought her a new abigail—Marie Duclos from Paris, whose hairdressing skill was exceptional! Marie and her own abigail Harriet were traveling in a second coach which contained Mary's five trunks and Tiffany's single bandbox. Yet despite being promised a wardrobe as large as her own Tiffany was quite cast down or, as dear Garnet would say, "deep in the dismals." Really, she must not look like a mute at a funeral when she was presented to her new stepfather! Garnet would not know what to make of her megrims! Garnet must not see them. Impulsively she turned in the direction of her daughter, but did not open her mouth to loose the spate of warnings that were massed on her tongue. Tiffany had fallen asleep!

The four spanking chesnuts were far, far too fleet. Eyes closed against threatening tears, Tiffany listened to the steady clip-clop of their sixteen hooves, hating the sound! It was indicative of the pace with which she was being whirled away from the abbey—or rather Pete Medina, whom she had seen only briefly that morning. He had been closeted in the music room, practicing, when she had arisen. Consequently, when her mother had arrived at the early hour of eleven, there had been no opportunity to exchange even one private word with him.

It had been impossible to tell from his expression whether he was grieved or shocked by Lady Mary' announcement that she had come to fetch her daughter. It had been impossible to say much of anything because her mother had been gushing on about the new house in Berkeley Square. She halted in her thinking, considering this new word. Had Lady Mary actually—gushed? Indeed, she had! She had gushed, giggled and turned this way and that, for all the world as if she were pirouetting before a mantua maker's mirror! Assuredly, the stamp of the mantua maker was broad on her back! She had never been more expensively turned out, not even in the early days of her marriage to Sir Matthew Prine. One could no blame her for rejoicing over this new stylish wardrobe. She had been a shabby little wren for such a long time naturally she reveled in becoming a peacock. It was wrong to resent her, but Tiffany could not help it!

Tiffany was positive she had never known the mean

ing of despair until those moments when she had stood directing Alice, her maid at the abbey, in the packing of her small bandbox while Lady Mary waited below, still chattering on and on and on about Lord Cavendish and Italy and Paris and gowns! Then she was down the stairs and it was as though last night had never taken place—but it had, it had, it had!

Though it had all the lineaments of a dream, it was not a dream. Her face yet burned from the touch of his lips, and her body remembered the strength of his arms when at length he had lifted her up and holding her high against his chest, he had borne her across the lawn. In the hall, he had looked at her concernedly, saying only, "You must divest yourself of that gown. It is wet through and you might take a chill."

She had nodded, wanting to say that she would never be cold again. The hot blood coursing through her veins and warming her cheeks precluded that. He had put his hand on her hair saying, "Tiffany." There had been wonder in his tone and his gray eyes had been alight with tenderness as he had added, "I will see you tomorrow morning."

"Yes," she had mouthed. She had wanted to say so much more but she could not. Yet, that morning she would have had the courage to speak, she knew it. But then her mother had arrived in her stylish garments, shining equipage, smart young servants; uttering her bright directions interspersed with her ceaseless, unfamiliar prattling!

Tiffany expelled a quavering sigh. If she could only beg Lady Mary to bear her back to the abbey, but it was impossible. That would mean she must also tell her mother what had occurred between herself and Peter, and she was not minded toward such a revelation—not to this stranger beside her, whose voice had taken on a peremptory note, when her daughter had asked to remain behind.

Lady Mary had not even inquired why she had wanted to stay. As far as Lady Mary was concerned, that was of no interest. Cousin Ellen too had looked surprised, aware that until that morning, Tiffany had been looking forward to her mother's arrival. A quick glance had showed her little flags of warning in Peter's eyes. Had he really whispered, "I will write to you," as he had handed her into the carriage? She had barely caught the words under her mother's stream of directives to the coachman. He had not looked regretful as he had waved at the departing coach. His face has been blank, his eyes blank. Had last night meant anything to him at all? Or had he merely responded to her most unmaidenly declaration? No, no, no, she could not believe that. Yet, it was equally difficult to believe that in a matter of a few moments— that was all it had been, really—he had changed from unfriendly acquaintance to lover. And now, when she might have known for sure, her mother had robbed her of that opportunity and of all happiness as well!

Five

"September is an empty month," Lady Mary had announced as they neared London. "No one of any importance is in town, which is why my dearest Garnet and I returned at this time. We wanted to get our house in order. The painting's at an end, and Mrs. Neal—a love of a housekeeper, my dear—will have seen to the disposition of the new furniture. I gave her the most *explicit* orders. I did not change all of it, only the master bedroom and the adjacent dressing room. I could not be expected to live intimately with another woman's taste, and the drawing room furnishings were not to my liking." She had shuddered. "Everywhere the eye fell, serpents coiled and crocodiles bared their teeth—Sphinxes, too. I do not mind Sphinxes, actually. Ibises too are quite unexceptional, but I am weary of the Egyptian motif. I did nothing with the library, I had a feeling Garnet would be most unhappy were I to touch it. Besides, it was under his direction that it was originally put together. It is in the Grecian style.

There are some fine authentic pieces of sculpture, as well as two beautiful libation jars. Garnet visited Greece in his younger days. His late wife left it alone, for which we must be grateful. I do hope you will like your new home, my love. Once you are settled, we shall concentrate on your wardrobe!

"Remember the silks I mentioned in my letter? We may now take them to Madame Le Gros. As for your riding habit, who do you think will fashion it?" Without waiting for a reply, she had clasped her hands saying worshipfully, "None other than Stultz of Bond Street! As you must know, he is a gentleman's tailor—except when it comes to riding habits. I have said it must be dark blue. My dear, you will cut such a figure riding in Hyde Park. Oh, Tiffany, if you only knew what it is, not to be faced with *scrimping!*"

For a moment, Tiffany had been vouchsafed a glimpse of the old Lady Mary, wistful and frightened. But then she had shaken her admirably coiffed head, saying lightly, "But I do not intend to think of the past. Oh, I am so happy! And I shall see to it, my dearest, that you will be happy, too!"

It had taken great resolution for Tiffany not to blast her mother's rosy dreams concerning hr future. However, much as she longed to tell her about her newfound happiness with Peter, Tiffany resisted that temptation. Not only was it a delight too precious to be shared, but she could not help remembering the warnings she had read in his eyes. Furthermore, though much of what her mother had told her passed into one ear and out the other, she could not help but be intrigued by the idea of a new wardrobe. It would be lovely if Peter were to see her in something besides her blue lutestring.

With that in mind, she could face the move to the city with more equanimity. Indeed, now as they made their way through London's streets, she was in a much better mood. She smiled a little as she peered from the coach window, befogged now with dust. Despite Lady Mary's contention that the town was well-nigh deserted, it seemed far from empty. To Tiffany's eyes, the drays, coaches, barouches, and curricles were as numerous as ever, and the noise nearly deafening! The curses of coachmen trying to maneuver their horses past slow-moving wagons, the cries of street vendors offering everything from cross and squealing pigs to succulent fruit pies to old clothes, pounded against her head; and in spite of her new resolution, tears rose to her eyes as amidst this cacophony, she heard the plaintive notes of a street fiddle.

Finally they reached Berkeley Square with its neatly fenced-in spread of clipped lawn, graveled paths and tall old trees. Moments later, the coachman drew up before an imposing early Georgian mansion on its south side. "Ah, here we are." Lady Mary smiled. "Is it not lovely?"

Accompanying her mother into a spacious hall, Tiffany had to agree. After years of dim, unfashionable lodgings on mean streets, to walk across marble floors and up a swirling staircase, to obtain glimpses of charmingly furnished rooms and to be brought into a bedchamber hung with new and colorful chintzes and filled with bright September sunshine was very pleasant. If she could never be entirely happy in a house that did not shelter Peter as well, at least she would find the waiting time more pleasant.

Lord Cavendish had not been at home when they arrived. However, an hour later he arrived, and to Tiffany, he proved a slight shock. She had spent the last four days listening to a lengthy recital both of his virtues and his heroism while commanding troops on the Peninsula and at Waterloo. If she had not expected the combination of Nelson, Wellington and Apollo that her mother described, neither had she envisioned a slightly built gentleman with more hair on his upper lip than on his head and that a brown gray which could only be categorized as mousy. Yet, if his face was not handsome, he did have an air of distinction, and what particularly commended him to his stepdaughter was his obvious adoration of his wife.

Each time he looked at Lady Mary, his eyes, which were a deep brown and quite his best feature, glowed with approval; and though he had been delighted to meet Tiffany, he had cleared his throat saying, "Er, my dear . . . though I do not wish to alienate you . . . I, er . . . well, my dear, I cannot think that your beautiful mother is cast into the shade—as she had feared—not at all. That is not to say—er—that you are not a very lovely young woman. I am sure my friends must agree. And"—he had taken her hand in both of his—"I shall be proud—er, very proud . . . very proud indeed to give the ball that will introduce my two beauties to the *beau monde*."

His only error and that a flagrant one—though Tiffany was generous enough to concede that he could not know her heart—was to remark that he had no doubt but that she would soon make a fashionable marriage to one or another high-placed young member of the ton. She had longed to tell him and her mother, who had stood by nodding agreement, that her heart and hand were promised to Peter. Such a revelation would have shocked them, but unfortunately, it was not true. Her heart might be in Peter's keeping, but her hand remained in her own possession exclusively. At the moment, her only hope was that this situation would be almost immediately resolved by a letter containing his official declaration. She had prayed that such a missive might be awaiting her upon her arrival—but it was not. Nor did she receive it the next day or the day after that.

It was fully fifteen days before Tiffany heard from Peter. In that period, the nights were the hardest, filled with gnawing pangs and pillow-pounding frustration—not to mention dreams of walking with him through moonlit gardens.

The days were easier to endure. As Lady Mary had promised, these were filled with visits to Madame Le Gros and to the shops in Soho Square. There one could find booth after booth filled with such intriguing items as ivory fans, morocco leather slippers and cashmere shawls; and, as Lady Mary explained, in buying them, one supported the widows and orphans of those who had died fighting in the Napoleonic wars. Consequently, it was an act of charity to make as many purchases as possible.

In the interests of the indigent, Tiffany found herself the possessor of a lace cap à la Mary of Scotland and another to wear under a broad-brimmed hat. Her mother had worn one like it on the day she had fetched her—which caused a pang until Tiffany remembered she was buying it for Peter's pleasure. Indeed, each time another item was added to the many she chose, it was selected with Peter in mind. By the end of the afternoon, Peter would eventually be admiring her in three bonnets, two with the new smaller shape and one a pink satin turban, ideal for carriage wear. He would also see a half-dress cap in embroidered muslin trimmed with lace and ornamented with a delicate spray of silken flowers. She had been quite unable to resist another cap fashioned from transparent gauze and trimmed with *British* blond, as opposed to its French equivalent; for, as the shopkeeper pointed out, French females were desirous of wearing British blond themselves, thinking it far superior to the native product. She also purchased a blue crepe shawl trimmed with knotted fringe, and Lady Mary had bought her a sable tippet and muff, for though the weather was uncommonly mild, certain sages had predicted a hard and snowy winter.

Tedious as they were, Tiffany was able to bear the ministrations of the mantua maker, an immense woman with a black mustache and hairs sprouting from big moles on chin and forehead, her shapeless body always encased in the same rusty black silk gown. She was accompanied by several emaciated young women, who trembled like aspens every time she barked out a command. Ranged round Tiffany, they all chattered in a nearly unintelligible French interspersed with sighs and hand-claspings, while they held up swatches and compared trimmings, treating Tiffany as if she were a wax mannequin. It was a process

71

which took hours but it was the end result that counted, and Peter would soon be able to appreciate her in a delectable evening gown of white lace over a white satin slip, its hem fancifully decorated with pink silk roses, its short puffed sleeves, striped with pink satin ribbons and slashed with lace insets. An evening ensemble, it would do very well for Peter's concerts. For his sake, she bore up under the fittings of several other equally fashionable gowns.

Thanks to the efforts of the seamstresses at the Le Gros establishment, the garments were finished in an amazingly short time and delivered in great round boxes to be unpacked in Tiffany's chamber by an admiring Marie Duclos.

Though her armoire was large, it was filled nearly to its capacity with morning dresses, walking dresses, her riding habit, and her evening gowns. Rows of kid shoes, sandals, and half-boots, some fashioned especially to match her ensembles, stood below them, while her chest of drawers was packed with exquisite shifts and night-dresses, as well as a host of other expensive trifles. If her happiness could have been measured solely in terms of feminine fripperies, she would not have traded places with a queen. Unfortunately, while filled to the brim, her cup was far from running over—mainly because nearly a fortnight had passed without word from Peter. Plaintively she remarked that she could not imagine why she had had no response to a letter full of news. "Surely," she had concluded, artfully disguising her real concern from her mother, "Cousin Ellen should have written before now."

Two days after she made that complaint, Lady Mary came into her room, an arch look on her face and a hand held behind her back. With the air of a conjurer producing a rabbit from a hat, she brought out two letters. "From the abbey," she said with a smile, an expression that vanished as Tiffany excitedly snatched them from her grasp.

"Lud," she remarked with some indignation, " 'tis easy to see you hold Cousin Ellen in as high esteem as your Mama."

72

"Of a truth, I do not," Tiffany assured her hastily. "Why would you think that?"

With a toss of her head, Lady Mary said petulantly, "You were certainly reluctant to leave the abbey. I did not know what to make of you that day."

"I . . . I was only surprised," Tiffany explained lamely.

"Indeed?"

Hearing the hauteur in her mother's tones, Tiffany felt a surge of annoyance. She could see that she was expected to read Cousin Ellen's letter out loud; and though certainly it must allay any suspicions that Tiffany might prefer her company to that of Lady Mary, she would far rather have perused her correspondence in private. She had little or no interest in anything her cousin might have written. It was the second letter with the slanting black handwriting scrawled across the envelope that claimed her whole attention. It could only be from Peter! A little tremor of fear passed through her as she realized that her mother would expect her to read his letter out loud as well.

"I am sure that second letter's from Peter. I am amazed. Why would he communicate with you?"

"Amazed, Mama? But we are friends," Tiffany said through stiff lips.

"Are you?" Lady Mary raised her eyebrows. "Yet, you've seen precious little of him in the last years. He has been from one end of the world to the other, has he not? Simon Esdras—how thoughtful of him to change his name, though I expect Ellen has not scrupled to let all Yorkshire know of his celebrity. It is fortunate that he's not played in London. I do hope that event will not take place until you are properly launched. Garnet is understanding, but it is so difficult to explain these things to strangers."

Tiffany stared at her in openmouthed consternation. "These . . . *things,* Mama? You are speaking of a world-renowned virtuoso!"

"Yes, yes, my darling, I am quite aware of his achievements but they'll hardly give him entrée into society. I do hope you've not encouraged him to visit us here. It would not be at all the thing, you know."

"Mama, how can you speak in such a way? Have you forgotten that . . . that . . ."

"I have forgotten nothing," Lady Mary said serenely. "I do have a debt to him that I mean to repay. But under the circumstances, my love, we must consider Garnet's position, though, of course, many good families do have exotic relations. But, no matter, do open your letters and let us hear what they have to say."

Cold chills were coursing through Tiffany's veins. She felt as though she were two people—one furiously angry at her mother and the other afraid. Neither emotion was familiar. To be both fearful and furious at Lady Mary was very strange. Yet, her mother had the power to spoil everything, to cut off the relationship between herself and Peter at its very inception. Still, there was no way she could refuse to honor what was, after all, a reasonable request.

With trembling fingers, she tore open Cousin Ellen's envelope and in a small, barely audible voice, began to read, "Dear Tiffany, I have just found time to answer your letter." Here her voice faded to a whisper as she stared uncomprehendingly at the next sentence. "Matters here have been so hectic, for on the very day of your departure, a messenger came from Prussia with a summons from Baron von Strelitz, who is attached to the court of King Frederich William of Prussia. Peter has been asked to perform at a special concert in honor of Prince Metternich."

"My dear," Lady Mary said sharply, "you must speak louder. I cannot hear you."

Dutifully repeating the sentence, Tiffany continued, "Naturally, he was most gratified and made arrangements to leave at dawn the next morning. Directly following that, he will travel to Spain where he will give concerts in Madrid, Barcelona, Seville, and Granada. Subsequently, he will be performing in Lisbon. I am much in the dismals for, as you know, I had looked forward to a longer visit—at least a month. Now it seems as if I shall not see him for another six."

With an effort, Tiffany looking up from the letter, managing to achieve a bland expression as she said, "Well, Mama, it seems as if your wish has been granted. You'll not need to worry about Peter's concertizing in London or visiting me here. Consequently, you and Lord Cavendish will be spared the embarrassment of pretending you are from home—in case he should be so untactful as to leave his card."

Lady Mary arose. Coldy she replied, "You are pleased to be ironic. I'll not chastise you for it, my dear. I put it down to your youth and inexperience. I am beginning to realize that I made a grave error in leaving you with Cousin Ellen. While I am much in her debt and while I truly love her, she has never been worldly. The shibboleths of society mean nothing to her, else she could not have behaved as she did. I do not intend, however, that you shall follow in her footsteps. You are young and beautiful, and can achieve a high position in our world. Consequently, I must tell you that I am very pleased that he will not be in London, at least not for the next few months. Furthermore, my dear, when you begin to take your rightful place in the sphere to which you belong by birth and breeding, I am sure that you will come to agree with me." Turning on her heel, she walked swiftly from the room—but not so swiftly as to prevent her daughter from seeing that her eyelashes were tipped with tears.

Knowing her mother, Tiffany realized that she fully expected a remorseful daughter to hurry after her, an apology trembling on her lips. However, she had no intention of making any such concession. Not only would it be against her nature, but it would be an admission that Lady Mary was right in what she had said concerning Peter. Thinking about it, she seethed with fury. She had never imagined that her mother could be capable of such base ingratitude. It had given her a shocking new insight into her character—or rather, the lack of it! Angrily, she thrust a fist into her lap and heard a crackling of paper.

Staring downward, she laughed. In her effort to reproach Tiffany, and at the same time make a telling and dignified exit, Lady Mary had quite forgotten that her now-despised Cousin Peter had written to her daughter. Hastily she opened the envelope that must contain her first love letter.

She thrilled at the salutation.

My dear little Tiffany,

My mother, I know, has explained the reasons for my sudden departure; and by the time you receive this communication, I shall, no doubt, be nearing my destination.

Needless to say, the summons was unexpected—but one which I could not refuse. It is, I might explain, typical of all that happens in the life of a performer. It is a most hectic and, at times, a painful existence, one which I should not wish to force upon anyone unaccustomed to its hardships.

Indeed, and I say this in all sincerity, I could never ask you to abandon a life of comfort and security for one of hasty departures, uncertain, even dangerous traveling conditions, uncomfortable lodgings. Many's the night I have passed in a barn and even under the open sky! However, be that as it may, I'll not say that I do not have regrets in making this decision or memories that I will always cherish. Yet, I am set on one path and you on another—toward a safer and happier situation than I could ever provide for you.

I beg that you will not think hardly of me—or feel that I have let you down. What I tell you comes only after mature and, I must assure you, regretful reflection. It is a decision at which I did not arrive easily, and I am sure I need not tell you how difficult a letter this was for me to pen.

The sight of moonlight in a garden will always arouse painful longings in my breast. Yet, I do know that I have made the wise—the proper—choice for us both, and I hope that you will come to agree with me. I hope, too, that I may count on your continuing friendship. The fact that our misunderstanding is at an end is a source of much joy to me, and, with all my heart, I thank you for your intervention at that time. Do not, my dear, think hardly of me. Yours—with all my best wishes for your happiness.

Peter.

She was conscious of a great roaring in her ears. The room seemed to waver in front of her and then to right itself. Looking about her a moment later, she was surprised to find everything as it had been before, when nothing really was—especially not herself.

Something terrible had happened to her heart—it had broken, and how might she continue to exist without it? She did not want to exist without hope or dreams, and these were gone, blasted because Peter did not want her. That was the essence of his message, no matter how gently, how persuasively he stated his case. *He did not want her!*

That moment in the garden had been just that—a moment. To have imagined that he had cared was a delusion. She could not think about that moment, but she could think of nothing else. Her disobedient mind was leading her back with incredible speed to the garden—to Peter!

She hid her face in her hands, rocking back and

forth in agony. He had never mentioned love—she recalled that now. It was she, she, she who had made that declaration. But he *had* kissed her, not once but many times and held her close against him; so close that she had felt the steady beat of his heart; so that she felt as if she had merged with him, had become part of him. It was a sensation that had remained with her all the days of their separation. But she had been wrong. Given his nature, which she knew to be gentle, he had been humoring her because he felt sorry for her. Sorry! Crumpling the letter into a ball, she ran toward the window and reaching it, thrust wide the casement. There was a breeze blowing. She would open her hand and let the wind have it, but her hand would not obey her. With a moan, she sank down on the floor and dropped the ball that had been his letter, smoothing it out so that she might read it again—all those kind cruel words!

A phrase from a tale she had read in *Ackermann's Repository* leaped to her mind: "He has seared my soul," the heroine had cried just before she had drowned herself in a lake. She now knew what that meant, she now knew the meaning of utter despair.

She read his letter again and a sob shook her as one of its sentences suddenly took on a new and sinister meaning. As far as he was concerned, she was naught but a memory to him, a rose petal pressed in a book. She was only a withered memento which would lose its fragrance and finally crumble into dust, and that, even before he set out for Spain—she was certain of it.

"What will I do?" she whispered. "How shall I find the strength to live without Peter?"

She had no answers.

"A ball and supper at the so beautiful Carlton House! *C'est merveilleux!*" murmured Marie Duclos as she stood behind Tiffany, placing the last of three white plumes into the nest of curls she had arranged. Her black eyes narrowed as she regarded her mistress's mirrored image. *"Ma foi!"* she exclaimed. "Why are you not excited? You must smile, *chérie,* else all of Marie's labors will be wasted!" She twisted her mobile features into an expression of comic melancholy. "*Le pauvre* Prince Regent, 'e is already *triste.* 'Is *jeune fille est morte* and it is not yet a year. 'E will wish to see the happy faces around him."

Tiffany was not in agreement with her little abigail. When one was depressed, the last thing one wanted to view was smiling faces, reminding one of lost happiness.

She gritted her teeth. She was forgetting her recent resolution. It had been born out of an agony that Dr. Noakes described as a species of low-grade fever. He had based his diagnosis on the fact that she had taken to her bed and lain there for three days in a darkened room, refusing all sustenance.

Through this method, she had hoped to fall into a decline and die. But her fasting had resulted only in hunger pangs which she had found impossible to ignore. On the fourth day, she had arisen with an interesting pallor, which had frightened her mother. It had disappeared, however, after the cook had sent up soup and fresh-baked scones. She was not sorry for that. She had lost all inclination to die, and after several hours spent reviewing the situation, her grief had turned to anger at Peter's inability to understand her.

He had mentioned the hardships a performer must endure, but he had failed to take into account that to anyone who loved him, such discomforts would not matter. Furthermore, she had endured considerable discomfort in Sir Matthew's household and she had survived. Peter should have known that she would have minded nothing as long as he was with her. In the days that followed her so-called recovery, she began to think less about the letter he had written and to ponder more on the one he had not—but which was nonetheless palpable between the lines of the crumpled missive she had secreted in her jewel box.

In effect, he had said he wanted his freedom. He did not wish to be burdened with a wife, and no doubt he had welcomed Lady Mary's timely arrival and the summons from Prussia as well. She had reached the uncomfortable conclusion that she had been very foolish. How could she have imagined that a few kisses meant that he had fallen in love with her! The suspicion that he had been humoring her rose again in her mind. He would not have the opportunity again—no one would! She would never again make the mistake of loving anyone. Never! But she could not help wishing that Peter would come back into her life so that she might have the chance to show him that her wounds had healed and that the protective skin that had grown over them was as hard as steel.

"Child, are you ready?" Lady Mary came swiftly into the room. She was looking very lovely in a black crepe gown. A square-cut neckline showed off her creamy white skin and she had chosen to wear a diamond and aquamarine necklace, the central pendant of which seemed to turn her gray eyes blue. Her golden hair was caught up in a coronet of braids which in turn was secured by a diamond comb.

"Oh, milady, how you are beautiful," Marie Duclos breathed.

"I—I am?" Lady Mary seemed to need reassurance. "Do you agree, Tiffany?"

"Oh, I do." Tiffany nodded. "I have never seen you look half so lovely."

"That is good. I do wish to be at my best tonight . . . the Prince, I wonder . . ." She frowned and shrugged. "But of course, it is a great honor. I did not know that Garnet was the Regent's good friend, one of the inner circle. He did not tell me so until tonight. I wish I might have known . . ."

"You speak as if it did not please you, Mama," Tiffany said with some surprise.

"Please me . . . Of course it pleases me, child."

Hearing uncertainty in her tone, Tiffany was moved. Here again was the old Lady Mary, gentle and timorous, the mother she had always sought to protect against Sir Matthew. They had protected each other in those days, she recalled. The new, almost overly confident woman she had seemingly become, was not to Tiffany's liking. She had been hoping that her mother would abandon that guise, and tonight it seemed to have vanished completely. She said, "I am sure you will be a great success. How could you not be? Besides, I've heard that the Prince admires ladies who are over thirty, though no one could believe that seeing you."

Lady Mary smiled but her voice remained edgy as she replied, "You are very kind, my dear."

"Truthful, Mama."

"Well, well, we'll not argue about it. Come, we do not want to be late. But I must assure you that the Prince does not—at least from what I have heard about him—he does not always confine his attention to women of mature years, such as I."

"Mature years!" Tiffany laughed. "Surely you are funning, Mama."

Lady Mary shook her head and then seemed to see her daughter for the first time that evening. "My love, how beautiful you do look! And the gown so becoming. I could not have wished for better. He will be pleased, I know he will. If—"

"Come," Tiffany interrupted with a laugh, "I cannot think Lord Cavendish will even notice me—not when he sees you."

"I meant . . ." Lady Mary turned away, saying tightly, "Never mind. We must be on our way."

As they drove toward Carlton House, Lady Mary's mood remained uncertain. She was either very quiet or hectically talkative. Lord Cavendish, however, seemed unaware of any strain. He himself, clad in a satin evening suit with a diamond order gleaming on his chest, beamed on his companions and was characteristically gallant.

"I shall be envied. I've never had the honor of escorting two such beauties. The Prince Regent, you know, is very partial to fair hair and blue or gray eyes. He has often deplored the fact that he lacks the ability to paint, for he insists that not even the great Sir Joshua

Reynolds has done justice to the English rose. And I am in agreement with him." He smiled fondly at Lady Mary. "Yet, I am determined that you must and will be painted, my love. I expect I shall give the commission to Sir Thomas Lawrence, though I could wish that George Romney were still living. He had a way with flesh tones, though I did deplore his penchant for painting women of ill-repute such as the late Lady Hamilton."

"Yet she was very beautiful," Lady Mary remarked. "When I was a little girl I once saw her—her coloring was exquisite."

With more severity than was his wont, Lord Cavendish said, " 'Tis a pity she had not the virtue to match it. It's singularly fitting that she died a drunken, blowsy wreck of her former self. Poor Nelson was besotted. Yet I expect that at thirty-four—her age when they met—she was still good-looking, though she could not have been a patch on you, my beloved."

Lady Mary seemed not to have heard that graceful encomium. Staring tensely out of the window, she said in a breath, "We have arrived."

As the coach drew to a stop, Tiffany felt her mother stiffen. She was sure she had guessed the reason for her nervousness and was sorry for it. Lady Mary was remembering Sir Matthew's ignominious withdrawal from society, his disgraceful suicide and Tom's arrest. Undoubtedly, she feared snubs and sneers, but, of course, that was ridiculous. If the ton could swallow a Letty Lade, who, before she wed Sir John Lade, had been the widow of Sixteen-String Jack, a colorful highwayman who was publicly hanged at Tyburn, it would certainly not look askance on her lovely, gentle mother. Furthermore, she had already received numerous invitations. Obviously Lady Mary was borrowing trouble.

Alighting from the carriage, Tiffany's concern over her mother was temporarily suspended. Even given her own uncertain mood, it was impossible to remain entirely unaffected by the excitement of the fashionable crowd massing in the courtyard. Flurries of laughter and chatter smote her ears; glimpses of satins and silks beneath wind-caught capes, the bright uniforms of the palace guard bathed in the radiance of the light shining from the tall windows of the great colonnaded building dazzled her eyes.

Obeying Lord Cavendish's warning about remaining close beside him, she clutched his arm as they joined the surging throng and entered the great hall. It was brilliant-ly lighted by myriads of candles in crystal lusters, in wall sconces, in candelabra, their flames reflected in the shin-ing marble surfaces of the massive pillars. Expertly guid-ed by her stepfather, she and her mother moved through opulent apartments, luxuriously furnished and hung with magnificent pictures. It was frustrating only to catch the merest glimpses of these treasures, but borne along by the rushing stream of people, she could not stop to admire them at length. Consequently, she emerged with a head full of kaleidoscopic imagery but with no clear recollec-tion of any specific hanging, cabinet, or jar. It did seem to her that there was an abundance of mirrors, an impres-sion that was heightened when on arriving in the hall just beyond the ballroom, she saw more mirrors at various points along its walls. Moving back, she blushed as she stepped on the foot of someone behind her, and heard a pleasant voice say, "I beg your pardon."

"Oh, no, it was my fault."

She turned to apologize just as her stepfather, also swiveling about, said, "By God, Ballard, but I thought your mother told me you were in France."

"I am just returned."

Tiffany found herself facing a tall young man as fair as she, but with the telling contrast of large, very dark brown eyes. He had a handsome aristocratic countenance, and he was dressed in a black satin evening suit of a cut that suggested the best of Bond Street tailoring.

"I should like you to meet my wife and my step-daughter," Lord Cavendish said, smiling.

Tiffany saw surprise flare in his arresting eyes. In the next few moments, she learned that he was Lord Ballard and that his late father had fought side by side with Lord Cavendish during a great part of the Peninsular campaigns.

With Lord Ballard still at her side, Tiffany entered the huge ballroom. Speechless, she stared at the crimson hangings, sparkling chandeliers, and the facing mirrors on either side of the apartment whose reflections endlessly multiplied the number of people present. On a platform hung in crimson silk, the orchestra was tuning up with a loud twanging of strings and scraping of fiddles. Several elderly dowagers had already appropriated the chairs provided for onlookers, and a few very plain young women had resignedly joined them. Most guests, however, stood in convivial little groups waiting for the moment when the Regent would arrive and the dancing begin.

"Miss Prine."

"My dear," Lady Mary whispered, nudging Tiffany, "Lord Ballard is speaking to you."

She started and looked up at him. "Oh, I—I fear I was abstracted."

"And well you might be." He smiled. "It's your first visit to Carlton House?"

"Yes."

"And how do you find it?"

"I am not sure. It is certainly luxurious and . . . and imposing."

"No expense has been spared," he agreed. "I am pleased, however, that you have reserved your opinion."

"And why should that please you?"

He regarded her out of twinkling brown eyes. "It shows that you are a discerning female. That is always refreshing."

She dimpled, pleased by his compliment but not quite sure how she must answer him.

He spared her the necessity by adding, "I do hope all your waltzes are not yet bespoke, Miss Prine."

"Not all of them," Tiffany murmured.

"Might I claim one, then?"

She had made up her mind not to dance, determined to join the dowagers in their chairs. But certainly it would be unmannerly to refuse the request of her stepfather's friend. "Of course. I should be delighted."

"It is I who am delighted. Which may I have?"

He could have had his choice of any, but in keeping with her recent decisions concerning gentlemen, she said hesitantly, "I believe, sir, that the third is unclaimed." Glancing at the fan on her wrist, she unfurled it, scanned its blank ivory spokes and closed it with a lightning move. "Yes, 'tis the third."

"Edmund!" A pretty dark-haired girl in puce satin, standing a few paces away, raised a beckoning hand.

He glanced in her direction and said regretfully, "I must go, but I shall be at your side the moment the third waltz is called." Bowing, he left her.

"That was very wise of you, my dear. Never be too available," Lady Mary whispered.

Tiffany had a rueful look for her mother. "I shall need to hide during the first two waltzes."

"I do not believe that will be necessary," Lady Mary said, her eyes on two young men who were making their way purposefully toward them. She was not mistaken. Almost before she knew it, Tiffany had agreed to take part in a cotillion and a quadrille, and the first two waltzes had also been promised.

"There," Lady Mary said. "I told you . . ." She paused, her eyes fixed on the double doors of the ballroom. Framed in that wide aperture was a heavyset man in the dark blue uniform of the King's Light Dragoons. If the color helped to minimize the broad expanse of a chest aglitter with diamond orders, the tight gray trousers were less flattering to his immense belly. Though his features were not unpleasant, the curly blond wig he wore made them appear singularly flushed and bloated.

"Egad," Lord Cavendish said in a low voice. "Damned if the Regent hasn't added another stone to his girth."

"He *is* heavy." Lady Mary's eyes were wide. "I never expected he would . . . would be such a size." She flushed. "I thought the cartoonists were exaggerating."

"He's a good-looking man, yet," Lord Cavendish

defended. " 'Tis not his fault the family's inclined toward corpulence."

Tiffany, after her first startled glance, had dropped her eyes. It would not do to stare at him. However, she too was reminded of those cruel caricatures that ornamented the windows of print shops. It seemed to her that they had all come perilously close to the mark. He was immense and his belly was so huge that the carrying of it must be a distinct strain. Yet his expression was affable. Stealing another glance at him, she saw that he was surrounded by a number of distinguished men and pretty women whom he was greeting graciously. Without knowing quite why, she felt drawn to him and then remembered that Lord Cavendish said the Prince had that effect on many people—even his most severe critics. She jumped as her stepfather said, "Well, my dears, I suggest we join the Regent."

"Oh!" Lady Mary seemed equally startled. "But he is surrounded. Should we not wait?"

"Better now than later. I want him to be in condition to appreciate your beauty."

"I doubt he'll notice me when he has Lady Conyngham at his side."

"Who can give you twenty years and has not half your loveliness," he laughed. "Yet, I am glad of the Regent's penchant for older females. Indeed, much as I admire his Royal Highness and count myself his friend, I could never accept the position of complaisant cuckold."

"Oh!" She gave him an affronted look. "How could you even imagine that I . . . I . . ."

"I do not imagine it," he assured her hastily. "I pray you'll not look so distressed, my love. I was but teasing."

"I—I fear I have little sense of humor about such matters. It is so wonderful to love and to be loved . . ."

Looking immensely gratified, he gave her his arm and holding out the other to Tiffany, he steered them toward the ever-widening circle about the Regent.

Tiffany noticed that he caught the Prince's eye almost immediately and received a smile and a nod. "Ah, well met, Cavendish, back from France, I see." His eyes remained on Lady Mary's face for a moment before he added, "I wonder that you did not remain on your honeymoon even longer."

"I was sorely tempted, I can assure you, Sire. Might I present my wife?"

"My Lady Cavendish," the Prince murmured. "I am delighted to meet you."

Lady Mary made a deep curtsey and was assisted to her feet by the Prince. "I am honored, your Royal Highness," she said in a mere thread of sound.

Tiffany, presented a moment later, fell into an even deeper curtsey than her mother and on rising found the Prince regarding her intently. There was a moment's hesitation before he said jovially, "Well, and this is your daughter, Lady Cavendish. You look scarcely of an age to have produced this young lady. Might one be indiscreet, my dear Miss Prine, and ask how many years have passed over your head?"

"I shall be eighteen in March, your Royal Highness."

"Ah . . . in March. You entered this world at the very edge of spring, a most felicitous beginning for the season."

She flushed. "Your Royal Highness is very kind."

Again she received an intent look. "And you are very lovely, my dear."

Tiffany's heart was thumping. She was both excited and daunted by his interest. Then she met the china blue stare of Lady Conyngham, who stood at his side. She was unpleasantly surprised by a hard, speculative glance. Feeling oddly discomfited, she shifted her gaze quickly. She had heard the phrase, "If looks could kill . . ." If there were nothing lethal in the lady's stare, it certainly contained a slap across the face.

"My dear Lord Cavendish." To Tiffany's relief, the Prince's eyes were once more on her stepfather. "I will say that you are doubly blessed in so attractive a family." He had a smile for Lady Mary. "I hope to see much more of both these fair damsels."

"I am honored, Sire." Lord Cavendish bowed. "I shall certainly do my best to arrange it."

As the Prince moved away from them, Tiffany noticed that a great many people were watching them, and that much of their attention seemed centered on herself. While some of the glances were quite as speculative as that which Lady Conyngham had bent upon her, others were merely cordial.

"My dear Tiffany," Lord Cavendish murmured. "I wonder if you know how very fortunate you are. 'Tis very unusual for the Regent to devote so much time to any one person, and that a young girl with whom he is not acquainted. I would say, my dear—" he turned toward Lady Mary, but whatever he was about to tell her, died on his lips as with a little moan and a helpless flutter of her hands, Lady Mary sank to the floor in a dead faint.

"Damn, what can be keeping the doctor?" Lord Cavendish muttered, as he sat beside Lady Mary's bed, absently patting her hand.

"There's a fog blown up," Tiffany told him, standing at the window.

Lady Mary moved restlessly. "It was the heat," she said faintly as she lay prostrate on her bed, still in her ball gown. Tiffany hoped it was a trick of the candlelight that made her eyes so shadowed and her face so pale. "It was warm in there, Mama."

"He always has his rooms overheated," Lady Mary whispered. "At least so I've heard."

"Yes, my love, that is quite true," her husband agreed. "He has a perfect horror of fresh air. Yet, I cannot think it was only the heat. You do not look at all the thing."

"A passing indisposition, I am sure," Lady Mary sighed. Regretfully she added, "I'd not have had you leave the ball, Tiffany, my dear. You looked so lovely and I am sure you should have had a great success."

"Do not think on it, Mama," she urged. "There'll be other balls, and certainly I'd not have enjoyed myself knowing you were ill."

"But that young man, Lord Ballard—so charming. I could see he was much taken with you. I hope you gave him your excuses."

Tiffany smiled reassuringly. "There was no need, Mama. He was at your side immediately, offering assistance. It was he who brought you the brandy."

"Oh, I—I did not see him."

"I think," Lord Cavendish said, "that you will be seeing a great deal of him in the future, my love. He has particularly asked if he may pay his respects—as soon as you are well enough to receive him."

"That should be passing soon," Lady Mary assured him. "You did not need to summon the doctor for a mere fit of the vapors, my dear Garnet."

"I shall be happier in my mind to have his reassurances as well as your own, my love." Lord Cavendish ran his hand through his wife's hair.

The gesture sent a host of unwelcome memories skittering through Tiffany's mind. She was in a moonlit garden and Peter . . . But she could not think about Peter, not at this moment, when other equally tormenting thoughts were plaguing her. Moving from the room, she paced restlessly up and down the corridor, then came to stand at the head of the stairs. Looking down, she stared at the hall floor. Its marble expanse brought an image of the Great Hall at Carlton House and she was in the ballroom with the Prince looking at her quizzically. *Quizzically?* Was that true? It hardly mattered. His sustained attention was what had mattered, and surely she had received that. Then her mother, who, given her current social ambitions, should have been ecstatic, had fainted.

"One has nothing to do with the other," Tiffany murmured reassuringly. But why was she seeking reassurance?

Because something had been wrong. Lady Mary had been distrait all the evening. Something had been preying on her mind—and she had been most reluctant to go to Carlton House.

Was that true?

Yes, she decided. Her mother had not wanted to

go—she had been tense, unhappy, frightened. *Frightened?* Was she right about that? Or was she refining too much upon it? She could not be sure. Yet, of one thing she was almost sure—her mother's swoon had been indicative of more than mere heat prostration. But what? The reasons for it evaded her. She started as the knocker on the front door slammed against the plate, sending hollow echoes through the hall. The doctor had arrived, and the butler's shadow was thrown upon the wall as, candle in hand, he went to admit him.

The examination did not last long, but it seemed an interminable time to Tiffany anxiously waiting outside the chamber. However, when at length the physician emerged with Lord Cavendish, she read nothing alarming in either of their faces, save that her stepfather was looking a little dazed.

"Dear me," he murmured. "This is very unexpected, Mr. Noakes." He added anxiously, "But her years, her health—"

"I see nothing that should trouble us."

"Well, I must say . . . well, I—I hardly know what to say. Please, will you come with me into the library, Mr. Noakes?"

"Sir?" Tiffany stepped forward. "Is Mama all right?"

"Ah, my dear, I did not see you." He smiled at her. "She's sleeping peacefully now, and there's naught should give you concern. I am assured that her indisposition is perfectly natural under the circumstances."

"The circumstances, sir?" Tiffany asked.

"She . . . well, er . . . well, you see, my dear, your Mama's breeding."

She stared at him incredulously. "Mama . . . a child?"

"Quite so, my dear." He swallowed and appeared very self-conscious. "Er . . . quite so."

"Oh, I do wish you happy." Tiffany reached out both hands to her stepfather, who grasped them warmly.

"I thank you, my dear. I am very happy, er . . . very happy. My first wife . . . so ill, you understand. After the death of our son, she could have no more children. I

90

never dreamed . . . God has been very good . . . very good to me. If you will excuse me, my love. Mr. Noakes and I . . . must talk."

She nodded. After they had gone, she sank down on a chair. She was more than happy—she was greatly relieved! All her strange amorphous fears had been for naught, and the shadow she had felt to be hanging over her mother's head had been lifted. Until that moment, she had not known how very fearful she had been. It was wonderful not to be frightened anymore!

Six

"It is uncommonly clear tonight." Tiffany stood at a window in the drawing room of her stepfather's house.

"You resemble a snowdrop in that gown," Lord Ballard remarked, surprising even himself with the romantic simile that had come to his lips. "I have never seen any female look half so lovely in white or, for that matter, in any other color."

She flushed with pleasure and could not resist the impulse to turn all the way around. "You like my new gown, then?"

His gaze was ardent. "Shall we say that I like what is in it? 'Tis a pity Byron never saw you."

"Byron?" she questioned. "Why should he have seen me?"

"Because he was partial to blonds, and undoubtedly you would have called forth his muse and become the subject of a poem. I would I might write one myself. I've tried, but my efforts . . ." He grimaced and laughed. "All for naught."

"Oh, dear Edmund, I need no poems from you."

"And shall have none," he said ruefully. "I am of a nature too prosaic to be wed to starlight."

She laughed. "You are not in the least prosaic. You are . . ." She paused provocatively.

"What?" he prompted anxiously.

"So many words are piling into my head that I do not know which to choose."

"Oh God, Tiffany, why is it not June already?"

"June? And my brideclothes not finished? I've had but two fittings."

"Blast all fittings! Damn your brideclothes! I should be happy to wed you, were you barefoot and in your shift."

"Sir!"

He gave her an anxious glance. "I pray I've not offended you."

"You never offend me, Edmund," she said softly. "From the very first moment we met, you've been kind, gentle and dependable."

"So might you describe a good dog," he said ruefully.

"Why, what can you mean?" she asked, wide-eyed.

His dark eyes were troubled. "I mean, you provocative little witch, that I am never certain of you."

"But we are betrothed."

"I have trouble believing it at times."

"Well, you may believe it." She moved closer to him and smiled. "I believe it."

"Do you?"

"Of course, you silly!" She turned away from him. "I wonder what is keeping Mama. I hope she's not suffered a sudden indisposition. It is getting late, and there'll be a crush of carriages in the street around the King's Theater. It would not do to be late for the concert."

"I have never encountered—a professional musician." Lord Ballard mused.

"They are quite like other people."

"And he is your cousin . . . the great Simon Esdras."

94

"The great Simon Esdras," she acknowledged. "Though I must warn you that when I see him, I shall address him as Peter."

"Peter. That is a name that sits oddly on him."

"Why?" She frowned slightly.

"From the engravings in the papers, he seems very foreign in appearance."

"Oh, he does, I know, but they have purposely emphasized his foreignness. He bears as much resemblance to the Clive side of his family as he does to the Medina."

He contemplated her for a moment in silence before saying, "You never mentioned him until the notices for his concert were posted. Yet, I begin to think you know him well."

Tiffany looked down. "I am better acquainted with his mother, my Cousin Ellen. It's a pity his concert could not have taken place at the end of April, so that the roads from Yorkshire might be cleared of snow and ice. I know she will be so disappointed at not being able to attend. And I should like to have you meet her. I know you'd love her as much as I do."

"When you lived with her, was her son in residence?"

"He is rarely in residence anywhere," she said dryly. "I do not imagine I have spent more than a week's time with him in my entire life."

"Ah. That is pleasant to hear."

"Do you not approve of musicians?" she demanded. "Or is it the mixture of blood that distresses you?"

"Neither the one nor the other. It is his likeness." Edmund's eyes lingered on her face. "If the artists do him justice, he is a good-looking man."

"And a dedicated violinist and twelve years my senior, my dearest Othello."

A slight smile played at the corners of his mouth, but his tone was grave as he replied, "Twelve years is not a lifetime, and I can give you eight years, myself."

"And will be my elderly husband within another two and a half months."

95

"Yes." His dark eyes seemed to capture some of the flame from the fire on the hearth. " 'Tis too long," he complained.

"It will pass," she said and fell silent staring at the burning logs. She was thinking about Peter. Had she known him so brief a time? Mentally she counted and the total was the same: that initial four-day journey from London to Yorkshire; his two days at the abbey; and then the night and morning of his return, five long years later. If one were to go by hours, she had known him far less than a week. And upon that brief span of time, she had been willing to build her life. How amazingly foolish she had been!

Suppose that he had encouraged her in her delusion, written the letter that must have brought her to his side? From the vantage point of eight months, she could laugh at her childish self and she could also be deeply grateful to him for that wonderfully wise and compassionate letter which she still retained. How gently he had dismissed her, and she had actually believed him cruel! He had not been cruel. In discouraging her, he had left the door open for another, a more rewarding relationship—with Edmund Ballard, Viscount Wray.

Dear, well-born, wholly English, entirely satisfactory Edmund of whom everybody approved—her stepfather, her mother and even the Prince Regent. Meeting them at a rout given by Lady Holland, he had gone out of his way to congratulate them on their coming nuptials. She had wondered how he had heard the news so quickly, and Edmund had reminded her that a notice had been inserted in the Morning Post of the previous day. Had Peter seen it, too? No, he had been in Portugal. But undoubtedly Cousin Ellen, alerted by Lady Mary, would have sent it to him. She wondered if he too would offer her his best wishes. She trembled a little at the audacity she had shown in asking Edmund to buy seats directly on stage. Would her presence prove a distraction?

She bit her lip. At nearly a fortnight past her eighteenth birthday, she was being very childish. Eighteen knew that kisses in a moonlit garden meant very little

More than one admiring gentleman had so far forgotten the proprieties as to attempt the same thing, before her betrothal to Edmund. She had coldly discouraged them, but she had no doubt but that their kisses might have proved exciting—quite as exciting as those she had received from Peter. No, that was not true. She had been very fond of Peter. But had she been as fond of him as she was of Edmund?

Edmund. It was amazing that he had become enamored of her so quickly. That was what she had been told by his sister Editha, whom she had met when she had visited the family at their estate in Shropshire.

"We had all imagined that Edmund would wed Hermione Strathmore," Editha had informed her. "We were expecting he must offer for her any day. And so, I am sure, was she. But I am ever so glad that he met you! Hermione is monstrously overbearing. Mama agrees with me. I know I shall adore having you as a sister, you are so beautiful."

"And I am delighted to have you as a sister," Tiffany had replied. She had spoken no more than the truth. She had found the girl's frankness delightful and she had been equally impressed by the widowed Lady Ballard. She was really wonderfully fortunate and it had all happened in seven months! It seemed inevitable. In that short time, she had become betrothed to a most eligible young peer; she had been taken up by the *beau monde*; she was feted and admired; and the dandies who sat in the bow window at White's had voted her an Incomparable! It was a marvel she had kept her head. That she had was because she did not attribute her good fortune to her scintillating personality or to the looks which everyone praised so highly, but rather to the kindness of the Prince Regent.

He had gone out of his way to be pleasant to her. He had, in fact, taken so singular an interest in her that some ladies looked upon her with ill-disguised suspicion. She frowned. Lady Conyngham's coldness to her was a by-word, and she knew it gave rise to malicious gossip concerning the exact nature of the Prince's interest. She wished they might have heard him on the day that he had said sadly, "You do remind me of my dearest Charlotte. She was of your coloring. Her early death was a bitter blow for a father, you know . . . yes, a bitter blow."

"Oh, I do know, Sire," she had cried impulsively. "I wish . . ." Then she had faltered into silence, because anything she might have told him regarding that same bitter blow could have provided nothing in the way of comfort.

He had taken her hand saying, "Yes, you are wise, my dear. There's naught anyone can say or do to bring her back. One can only have regrets for what was not said in life—or done. But let me not burden you with my old guilts. 'Tis a pleasure just to look at you. A pleasure and a comfort as well."

There had been several such encounters. Enough so that the risibilities of a rising young caricaturist had been stirred, and in the window of one of the print shops there had appeared a devilishly amusing cartoon of the Prince Regent dandling a baby on his lap—a baby with her features!

Her mother had been dreadfully disturbed; but her stepfather, after a brief explosion of anger, had laughed, saying resignedly, "Nearly all of the Prince's cronies have been speared by those wounding pens."

"And can nothing be done to stop them?" Lady Mary had retorted sharply.

" 'Twould be folly to try. The Prince learned that lesson long ago, my love."

Edmund, however, had taken a different view of the attack. He had sought out that luckless artist and horse-whipped him! She shuddered. That action had surprised and disturbed her. Edmund was usually so gentle that she would never have suspected him of harboring such animosity in his breast. It had given her a new insight into his nature and had even made her a little afraid of him but that, of course, was nonsense. There was no reason to fear Edmund, who had been kindness itself from the very first, when he had brought the brandy to Lady Mary on the night she had fainted.

He had called the next day and in a very short time, he had become a regular visitor, sending Lady Mary and herself marvelous bouquets of roses and orchids from his hothouses at Wray. There had been others who had pursued her, but none had been as persistent or as attractive as Edmund. Was it that attraction, or his sheer persistence that had won her? She sometimes thought she had agreed to wed him because everyone seemed to think that she must. Even her abigail had waxed lyrical over the "so elegant, trés charmant young gentleman." But she had not listened to those who had praised him. They had not swayed her. She had accepted him because she enjoyed being with him, because she had always found him charming. And there was another factor that had moved her in his direction. He adored her. He made that patently evident. It was wonderfully pleasant to be adored rather than adoring. But she did adore Edmund, she was sure of that!

"Ah, my dears, I am indeed sorry if I kept you waiting, but I am ready now and Garnet says we must be on our way." Lady Mary, followed by Lord Cavendish, joined them. Tiffany was pleased to find her mother looking her best. Though there remained but some five weeks until her time, her condition was admirably concealed by the fashionable fullness of her green satin gown with its overlay of silvery net. Her fair hair was dressed in a coronet of braids through which were threaded small pearls and peridots. Of late, she had been a little pale, but excitement had brightened her coloring; and as Edmund was quick to assert, she presented a ravishing picture, one which must certainly take the eye. Peter might not notice her in her white gown. But surely, he would see Lady Mary, and in recognizing her, his eyes must drift to her daughter and her daughter's fiancé. Once she caught his glance, she would move even closer to Edmund and smile up at him. Pride would thus be satisfied.

As Tiffany had anticipated, the streets in the vicinity of the King's Theater were extremely crowded. The first concert of a famed virtuoso—an Englishman, besides, and one who would play the relatively new and difficult Concerto in D by Ludwig von Beethoven—brought out the musical fraternity and their noble patrons, the one to fret and cavil in the gallery, the other to whisper and preen in the boxes. Though Tiffany had expected that only a very few would sit on the stage itself, she found that there were several rows of seats on all three sides. However, with a sagacity she hurried to praise, Edmund had bought a block of tickets to the left of the stage, not wanting to sit facing the performer's back. Their seats were located in the middle of the third row which was, a gratified Lord Cavendish said, one of the most satisfactory of locations!

How satisfactory, they would never guess, Tiffany thought as she took her place. There was now no doubt in her mind but that Peter must see the four of them. What would he think? Would she read surprise in his gray eyes? Would he smile or frown? Or would he pretend not to see her at all? She would soon find out, for they had been shown to their seats only minutes before he was due to emerge from the wings.

The orchestra was already ranged along the stage. She stared curiously at the musicians. She had never been so close before. To her surprise, she found that though from the house they appeared very staid and dignified, they were actually laughing and muttering to each other. Occasionally a random bar of music would be performed on one or another instrument, an agreeable contrast to the eternal testing of strings and the tentative squeaks or brays from the horns. Scanning the hall, she saw that it was filled to capacity and that extra chairs had been brought in at the ends of rows. There was considerable chatter and laughter from all sides of the auditorium, and she could only hope it would die down once the conductor entered. It would be dreadful if the audience were as inattentive as at the theater, when some of the actors' voices were drowned out. Then she stiffened, for on glancing toward the top of the house, she saw a man whose shock of bright red hair reminded her unpleasantly of Tom Prine's vivid locks. He was too far away for her to distinguish his features—but it could not be Tom, surely. He had no funds to expend on tickets. She grimaced. In recent months, Lady Mary had received three begging letters from him. She had sent him generous amounts on two occasions and had fully intended to honor his third request had not Lord Cavendish discovered the letter.

He had gently admonished his wife. "You've a soft spot for that scapegrace. But, my dear, you must cease to encourage his demands, else he will be your pensioner forever."

"But I cannot see the lad starve."

"His kind never starves," he had assured her grimly. "Nor will he trouble you again." So saying, he had pocketed the letter, unmindful of his wife's soft protest, "But Garnet, I want to help him."

Since that time, there had been no word from Tom.

Tiffany was thankful that her stepfather had asserted himself; she could not understand her mother's willingness to accede to Tom's requests. Lady Mary had never liked him as a child and she had often told Tiffany that she had always expected he would come to a bad end. Tiffany shook her head. There were times when her mother's actions confounded her. She shrugged the unpleasant memories of her stepbrother away as a resounding note from a violin brought her attention back to the stage.

The first violinist, instrument in hand, had taken his place and he was now tapping his bow against his violin. She was gratified to notice that a great deal of the noise was dying down. Another glance at the audience revealed that it had grown intent and expectant.

And now Peter was entering from the wings.

At the sight of that tall elegant figure which she had not viewed in such a long time, she felt a painful throbbing in her throat. She wanted to lean forward, she wanted to attract his attention in some way. But she sternly quelled that ridiculous impulse! Her breathing, she found, had grown less steady, and there were odd little fluttering sensations coursing up and down her body.

He was dressed all in black, save for his snowy cravat. How beautifully his dark hair waved back from his forehead—he looked so very handsome. He was glancing at her side of the stage! His slanted eyes under his dark, winged brows seemed to be fixed upon her. Yet she caught no gleam of recognition in them. His gaze was blank, unseeing, almost as though he were looking inward rather than outward!

"So that is your celebrated relative," Edmund whispered.

She subdued a start, simply nodding. She had forgotten that Edmund was beside her; she had forgotten why she had been so eager to attend the concert, why she had wanted to sit on the stage; she had also forgotten that the reason she had wanted Peter to look in her direction was so that he might see her smiling adoringly at her fiancé. She had not glanced at Edmund once, and she did not look at him now. She was unable to take her eyes from Peter, and she now knew that she had been living on the periphery of memory, not daring to penetrate into the fastness where the image of Peter was yet contained. It was no use deluding herself. To see him again was to suffer all the torments she had believed ended. They had not ended. As a child of twelve, she had given her heart to Peter Medina; though he might scorn that offering, it yet remained firmly in his possession.

She was appalled. She could not love a man who cared nothing for her. She . . . Her clamòring thoughts must be banished. He was holding his violin in readiness and the unfamiliar strains of the concerto were in her ears. In spite of her inner turmoil, she listened to the opening passages with appreciation; they were beautiful. She had always loved any work of the famed Viennese composer—not Viennese, German. Her random musings must end, for Peter was tucking his instrument beneath his chin; and now as the orchestra muted its tones, he drew the bow against the strings. How his slender fingers vibrated at the top of the violin!

A tone of incredible sweetness filled her ears—rising, falling, wandering through intricate melodic mazes and emerging from them to slide easily up to incredible heights of sound and then to fall as easily into other enchantments. She had the impression she was being led out of herself, as though some shadowy part of her were following the sounds through shimmering, rose-hued corridors. Tears pricked her eyes. She did not understand the feelings his playing unleashed. She knew only that it worked upon the innermost recesses of her soul until she felt purged of all petty emotions. Then, she remembered his letter, and now, at last, she understood all he had not said. It was not his longing for freedom that had taken him from her, it was his music. That had been her rival, seducing him, beguiling him, drawing him out of the moonlight, away from her, away from all mundane ties into the celestial spheres of melody—and it was only right that his music should have the prior claim. She felt humbled, diminished by the experience of hearing him, and yet, at the same time, her sense of being borne to the heights remained. There was no doubt but that he was a master. She did not need to depend upon her own awareness for that, she had only to look about her at the rapt and silent audience. Yes, even the rude and critical fraternity of the galleries was listening attentively to that alternately tender and powerful sound.

She felt as though she had returned from a long journey to an unknown land when the music finally ceased and the violinist stood pale, spent and actually diminished, as though an intrinsic part of him had ceased to exist. There was a moment of utter silence and then a deafening roar of approval. Cheers, coupled with the stamping of feet, seemed to shake the old house. Flowers rained about him as he smilingly but wearily bowed. The members of the orchestra bowed, too, and the conductor shook hands with Peter. He was called back again and again and then finally, he was gone, looking neither to the right nor the left. She was not disappointed. Her initial plan now filled her with shame. She was reluctant to go back and see him, but that, of course, could not be avoided. Her mother and stepfather had been equally entranced by his artistry; she had seen tears in Lady

Mary's eyes. Momentarily she had resented the fact that her mother had been similarly moved by his music. And then again, she was ashamed of herself. She must be pleased that he had the power to stir the senses of all who heard him.

"I must say that your cousin's a fine musician," Edmund murmured. "A superb technique. Quite out of the ordinary, I should think."

His comment infuriated her. Considering the magnificence of his performance, that praise seemed small indeed. However, her common sense quickly informed her that her feelings were again unjustified. Edmund's nature was cool. He was never one to express himself in superlatives nor was he particularly fond of music. "Yes, he is very fine."

"I expect we must go back," he sighed.

"Do you not wish it?"

"I cannot say that I do, my dear. I never feel quite at home in . . . artistic circles."

She heard a distaste in his tone that annoyed her. "You were mentioning Byron."

"That is different. George is one of us and—" He broke off, reddening. "You must forgive me, my dear. I forget that he is your cousin. I pray you'll not impale me with your glance, my love." He gave her a tender smile. "I *am* sorry. Come, let us go on back."

Coveys of words had formed on her tongue. She had been ready to loose them, but his hasty apology had made that impossible, and what, after all, could she have said? Edmund's attitude was typical of his class, there was no changing it. Professional musicians were lumped with actors and even opera dancers. She must swallow her anger. She must recollect that he was very dear in other ways.

The passage beyond Peter's dressing room was full of people and Lord Cavendish, looking down at his wife, said anxiously, "I think it were best, my dearest Mary, that I find some official to shepherd us through the crowds. I cannot think that you should wait out here."

She gave him a grateful smile. "If you might," she murmured.

"I shall be back momentarily."

As he hurried off, Edmund offered his arm to Lady Mary. "Let us stand against the wall out of the way." He paused, startled by a string of epithets uttered in a deep, feminine voice. Conversation about them was momentarily silenced as a tall young woman clad in bright, tawdry silks, flounced forth from the dressing room, her face contorted with rage. She was followed by a small, dark man clad in a servant's black. He closed the door behind him hastily, looking greatly embarrassed. Putting a hand on her arm, he was thrust back with a telling and—from his pained expression—hurtful jab of her elbow. Pushing him aside, she clutched the doorknob, rattling it. "Damned Jew!" she yelled.

"Please, Madame," the little man moaned. "The maestro—"

"To hell with the maestro!" she screamed. "He knows me." Pounding on the door, she cried, "You know me. Don't tell me you've forgotten me, Jew!"

"I'm sure there's many as knows you, doxy," mocked a voice from among the onlookers.

A chorus of laughter followed his comment and was topped by curses so virulent that some of the women gasped and put their hands to their ears.

" 'Ere!" said a burly man who made his way to her. "Ye cannot stay 'ere'n make a commotion, my girl. Out where ye belong!"

She glared up at him furiously, but evidently his height and bulk gave her pause. With a toss of her head, she started pushing her way through the throngs.

"Tiffany!" Edmund said in an admonitory whisper. "Why will you look at that strumpet? Stand back."

She had been watching the altercation in stunned amazement. "She—" She broke off as the woman, coming near them, suddenly halted, staring at Tiffany.

Her eyes widened, and, if possible, she looked even more infuriated than before. "You!" she mouthed. Her hand half rose, then fell to her side as Edmund moved forward, a protective arm about Tiffany's waist. With another curse, she resumed her progress through the corridor and was lost to view.

"Oh, God." Tiffany pressed a knuckle against her lips.

"Child, what's the matter? Why did that creature look at you like that?" Lady Mary gasped.

"I . . . I know her," she breathed.

"You know her?" Edmund repeated incredulously. "How might you know such a trollop?"

"It was years ago. She ran away from the abbey."

"She was one of Ellen's servants?" Lady Mary inquired.

"Yes," Tiffany said quickly. "One of her servants." She could not tell them the truth—could not say that this was Sara Wingfield, whom a twelve-year-old child had betrayed out of love and pity for her cousin Peter.

"Ah, that's why the wench was attempting to see him," Edmund laughed lightly. "His youthful follies pursuing him, and at such a time! How inconvenient. Yet 'twere better to have paid her off, I'm thinking."

"Paid her off?" Tiffany questioned.

He reddened. "No matter, my dear. I keep forgetting that I am in the company of an innocent."

She was further confused by that remark, but she could not ponder on it. She was still too appalled by Sara who looked not unlike the whores who used to stroll the street in front of Mrs. Bowes's lodging house. She had recognized her immediately she had come out of Peter's dressing room. However, she had not expected that Sara would know her. Judging from her furious glare, she remembered that it was Tiffany who had led Peter to the abbey all those years ago. Yet how had she recognized her? She had been only twelve, and surely she was much changed. Recalling that fiery stare, she shivered. If only she had not stood where the girl could see her. Yet even if Sara had seen Tiffany, she could do naught to harm her.

Before she could think on it further, Lord Cavendish strode back to them, accompanied by the small man in black. "This is Roberto, Mr. Esdras's valet. He will take us to see his master," he explained. "Lord, Lord, it took some doing," he muttered as they followed the valet. "Yet, I am glad that I'll not leave for Ireland until the morrow. I'd not have missed the concert, and I shall be honored to meet your cousin, my dear Mary."

Tiffany, overhearing these words, warmed to Lord Cavendish, contrasting his remarks with Edmund's chill comments and what she now realized was the suggestion that Peter must have contributed to the downfall of his so-called maidservant. She smiled wryly. Edmund had called her an innocent—by which he meant ignorant of certain conditions in the city. Poor Edmund! How he would have writhed had he known the extent of a knowledge gleaned from Tom, as well as through her own observation during sojourns in such lodging houses as Mrs. Bowes's. She winced, wishing she had not recalled either Tom or Mrs. Bowes, which brought to mind again the man with red hair. Tom's hair had been such an unusual color; but no, he would have no reason to come to the concert. He had never liked music. Banishing him from her thoughts, she fixed her attention on the portal of Peter's dressing room.

A number of fashionable people were emerging as Tiffany's group entered, and Lord Cavendish was hailed by a friend, who regarded him in some surprise. "I thought you were in Ireland, Garnet."

"I start for the Irish coast tomorrow."

"I wish you had not to go," Lady Mary murmured. "Bother the estate!"

"I shall be back soon enough, my love." He followed her across the threshold and Tiffany, clinging to Edmund's arm, felt bubbles rising and exploding in her throat as she looked about a large and crowded room. Laughter and chatter in several different languages filled her ears. Peter, she noted, was surrounded. A queer little pain arose in the vicinity of her heart as she saw that several very attractive women were standing very close to him. A few paces distant, a slender, flame-haired beauty in gold silk was looking at him with a proprietary air.

There was something about her that reminded Tiffany Sara. She had the same vivid coloring and striking a pearance.

She wondered what had taken place between Pet and Sara. Judging from her curses and her spate of ang words, he had not recognized her—but he must ha known her! How angry he must have been. Thinki about it, her own anger rose. How had Sara dared come back on the night of his triumph? Had she not do enough to him? How had she dared believe he would s her?

"A surprise, you promised me a surprise." Tho words came back to her. They had been spoken by t young, greedy Sara, wheedling a gift from Peter. It mu have been in the hopes of money that she had con again, and he had sent her packing, as she so rich deserved!

She tensed, her attention arrested by the woman gold. She seemed to know some of the men congratulati Peter. She spoke to one of them in French and to anoth in a language that Tiffany did not recognize. She turn back and looked at Peter with an affectionate smi A coldness arose in Tiffany's breast. Could that woman his wife?

"Peter, my dear." Lady Mary's tones drifted back her, and she found that her mother and Lord Cavendi were at his side.

"Come." She caught Edmund's arm and moved fo ward to join them. As she raised her eyes to Peter's fa her feelings crowded in on her. There was so much s wanted to tell him—but none of it did she want to say front of all the people present, in front of the golden la still hovering in the background. She shot a glance her—she was smiling at Peter. How dared she look him as if he were her particular property? Now, Pete gaze was on her. The words rushed to her lips, but all s could produce was a subdued, "Peter."

"My dear Tiffany," he said cordially, "how ve good to see you again."

"And you . . . I . . ."

Before she could say more, he had added, "My mother writes that you are soon to be wed."

"Yes, that is true. My fiancé, Lord Ballard." Once she had dreamed of making this introduction. In that dream, she had been assured and triumphant. She had not glanced at the floor, she had not spoken in the merest whisper, she had not wished she were a thousand miles distant.

There was a polite exchange of greetings followed by Edmund's gracious compliments, to which Tiffany was able to add her own. But all the while she was chiding herself because she had no way of conveying all that his music had meant to her. All too soon, she heard Lady Mary's gentle reminder that they must leave, and then, they were turning to go and others were coming to take their place. At the door, Tiffany could not resist a backward glance—and she caught Peter's eye. She bit down a gasp. She felt pierced, invaded by the intensity of that look. The intensity and the yearning—a yearning which she knew must be duplicated in her own eyes. Then there was Edmund's hand on her arm, drawing her forth into the passageway.

Dutifully she had accompanied her fiancé from the theater, but she had not wanted to go. Inside of her was a Tiffany who was running back and throwing herself into Peter's arms, begging him to hold her and never release her. Oh, if she might have followed that phantom self? The woman who had smiled at him no longer intimidated her. There was no mistake. Peter did care about her, and she had to see him again. There was another concert on the morrow, but they were bidden to Lady Gray's house. She, her mother, and Edmund, and—

"Taffy!"

She started. There was a large crowd around them and someone in it had called her.

"Taffy is a Welshman . . ." But Tom was the thief— Tom, whose teasing voice rose up in her memory. She recalled the man with red hair, and even as that vision arose before her, a tall, husky red-haired man stepped forward to grin down at her.

"Tom," she mouthed.

His grin broadened. "Sir Thomas Prine, at your service," he acknowledged, cocking an eye at Lady Mary, who had stiffened and paled. "Might one bid you a good evening, milady?" He smiled, adding in a low voice, "I'm a bit down on my luck. I am in hopes that you might help me."

Her eyes flickered from Tom to the tall figure of her husband who was striding toward them. Tiffany saw that her mother looked more frightened than indignant as she gasped, "I—I have done all I can for you."

"All?" he demanded gruffly. "I beg to disagree with you, my lady. I—"

"What are you doing here?" Lord Cavendish confronted him, looking, Tiffany thought, like a small bantam cock confronting a barnyard rooster. However, he was a very valiant bantam. He continued, glaring up at Tom, "I told you when I last saw you that you were not to show your face anywhere in the vicinity of my wife. You told me you would take what I gave you and go to America. Why are you still here? I must tell you that if I see you anywhere near her again, I'll have you transported. I might mention that this is not an idle threat. Now, will you be gone? Or shall I summon a constable?"

Fury burned in Tom's eyes, but he moved aside as Lord Cavendish took his wife's limp arm and led her toward his waiting carriage.

For once, Tiffany was glad of the tall and protective presence of her fiancé. She was even more pleased to settle down in the carriage and drive off.

"Damn and blast the little wretch! If I could get my hands around her throat, I'd twist her head off," a tall, red-haired woman muttered.

Tom, staring after the departing carriage, turned an inflamed eye in her direction. "And do you know them, too?" he inquired gruffly.

Her hot eyes fell upon him. "And what's that to you, sir?" she asked insolently.

He was surprised. Despite her looking like a drab

from the Covent Garden bagnios, her tone was cultured. "As it happens, my good wench," he said in accents no less refined than her own, "I too have a passing acquaintance with them. And obviously I have no more reason to rejoice in that than yourself. Shall we trade stories before a cozy fire, with a draft of Blue Ruin to warm us further?"

Her eyes were appraising. "Where would we find that—cozy fire, sir?"

"My lodgings."

"That will cost you money," she returned.

"I've precious little of that, my sweet jade, but I've a plan whereby I can acquire more . . ."

She gave a husky laugh. "I don't fill my gullet on promises, sir." Then her eyes narrowed. "But do you know the little witch in white?"

"Well."

"How well?"

"Well enough to have called her sister, once. Her dam was wed to my father."

"Ah." She sauntered up to him and slipped her arm through his. "I'll come with you." She smiled.

Seven

The next evening, the passage outside of Peter's dressing room was as crowded as it had been the night before. Tiffany with Marie Duclos at her side, a small, dark, and disapproving presence, made her way to the door. Despite the hauteur easily discernible in the abigail's eyes, Tiffany had her to thank for her swift progress along the corridor. Her shrill, French-accented speech, her air of accompanying a lady of quality, and a remarkably sharp elbow were all eminently helpful as was Tiffany's own appearance. Her furred cloak with its deep hood half concealing her face was in the latest style and as she moved, provocative glimpses of a blue satin gown were revealed. A blue velvet reticule swung from her wrist and her little kid slippers, also blue, were finely crafted. A faint but beguiling scent arose from her person, and though she walked quickly, she had an air of dignity about her.

Yet now that she had reached the door and Peter

113

was only a knock away, the enormity of her actions dulled her excitement. She had told so many falsehoods that her audacity amazed and daunted her. The first of them had been spoken even before she had retired last night.

"I do feel rather queasy," she had said to her mother, as they parted at the head of the stairs.

"I am sure you will be yourself in the morning," Lady Mary had replied equably. " 'Tis only the excitement of the concert. He did play so well, did he not? I do wish Ellen had been here. I must write her about it."

She had gone on to discuss the concert and no more had been said about Tiffany's indisposition. But the following morning she had pronounced herself too ill to rise or even to drink the cup of tea Marie brought her. That had been the most trying aspect of her deception—her steadfast denial to a demanding stomach. She had taken only water, and she had remained in her bed all the day, curtains drawn against the brilliant sunshine. Toward evening she had been forced to placate her worried mother by imbibing a potion which had tasted vile and had almost made her really ill. However, the discomfort was small when she contemplated her victory. All unsuspecting, her mother and Edmund had gone off to Lady Grey's banquet, and she could, with the grudging aid of her reluctant abigail, put her plan into action.

Marie had had a host of objections. "If you should be seen at the concert by one or another friend of your family . . . you cannot ensure their silence."

"I have thought of that, Marie. I shall not be seen because I shall not attend the concert, and I shall bribe the doorman at the stage entrance to let me in. I must see my cousin."

"And do you not imagine that others besides yourself will wish to see him?"

"I shall wear my hood up—he will see me alone."

"Tu es folle!" Marie intoned. "No good will come of this venture, I feel it deep in my bones. You will be found out and I shall be dismissed."

But in the end Marie had capitulated, though not without the persuasive gift of a gown she particularly coveted and a few trinkets of minor value.

Now, as Tiffany raised her small gloved hand to knock on the door, she too was uncomfortably positive that she had erred, but it was too late to turn back. He would have had her note; he would be expecting her. She doubled her fist and brought it down on the panel. The door was opened and she stepped across the threshold, coming to so sudden a stop that Marie, who was just behind her, only narrowly avoided falling against her.

Peter was not alone. There were several people talking to him, but she barely looked at them. Her eyes were all for the woman who stood in the circle of his arm, the woman in gold. She was not in gold tonight. Her gown was green and of some clinging material that outlined her tall, beautiful shape and was cut low over her breasts. It was a color that was almost a perfect match for her eyes. She had the same coloring as Sara Wingfield—and she was standing so close to him!

Tiffany longed to dash out of there, but she did not. Instead, she joined the circle, smiling valiantly at Peter and adding her own phrases to the chorus of congratulations directed at him.

He greeted her with a smile of his own. But there was no trace of the look she had surprised the preceding night. He was pleasant and gracious, thanking her for her kind words, and adding, "Blue is certainly your color, my dear Cousin Tiffany." His eyes admired her dark cape with its sable trimming. "You are quite the fashionable lady."

"I thank you," she said. "You'll not be giving another concert here in London, Peter?"

"No," His eyes flickered away from her face as he smiled to someone who was evidently behind her. "I shall leave for Yorkshire soon."

"But the roads," she protested wearily.

"I shall wait until they are dry, of course," he replied.

"You must give my love to Cousin Ellen."

"I shall do that with pleasure."

She could not bear to look at him, could not bear to hear his polite answers, could not bear to face the stranger who stared at her from his eyes—the stranger whose arm had never once moved from the waist of the woman beside him, the woman who smiled at her nestled in Peter's grasp.

Tall, russet-haired, green-eyed—Sara's coloring, her height and grace, but much more beautiful. That was the type of female Peter admired, and obviously she was his mistress. She could no longer look at either. Eyes downcast, she said, "I must bid you good-night, Peter."

"Good night, my dear." He took the hand she had not offered and brushed it with his lips—they felt so cold!

She left his dressing room without a backward look, moving hastily down the corridor, followed by a silent Marie. Coming out of the stage door into the frosty air she relished the coolness against her burning cheeks. The hackney she had hired was waiting around the bend of the street, a little less than a block away. She had walked about half the distance when a tall man stepped from the shadows and caught Marie by the arm.

"Nom de Nom!" Marie exclaimed angrily. "What is this, you—" Whatever she might have said died away as, with a lightning move, he clipped her chin with his large fist. She fell without another sound.

"Marie!" Tiffany cried. Shock, momentarily immobilizing her, she stared in horror at Marie's assailant, but it was too dark to see his features. With another cry, she turned to flee, only to be caught and held in powerful arms. A hand was clapped over her mouth, stifling her scream.

"My dear Taffy," murmured an all-too-familiar voice. "Well met by moonlight. 'Tis a paraphrase but more apt, do you not agree? Come, then, my dear."

She was vaguely aware of someone else moving in the shadows as Tom removed his hand. She started to scream but the sound was once more stifled by a damp ill-smelling cloth thrust against her face. The odor seeped into her nose and mouth making her dizzy and sick. Even while she strove to escape the pressure, the cold moon overhead blurred and vanished in blackness.

There was a gentle hand on his shoulder. "Maestro," a regretful and nervous voice murmured.

Peter, opening drowsy eyes, was outraged. He glared at his small valet. "I thought I told you, Roberto, that I wished to sleep until I awakened. Without your assistance!"

"Si, maestro," Roberto said apologetically. "But your cousin awaits. . ."

"My cousin!" Peter sat bolt upright staring at Roberto incredulously. Her persistence angered him. Why was she pursuing him? Had she no pride? He was not prepared to see her at this moment, when he had yet to gather his thoughts. "You should have told her—" he began.

"Pardon, maestro, but it is Lady Cavendish who wishes to see you."

"Mary? At this hour?" It occurred to him that with the draperies drawn, he might have judged it to be earlier than it really was. "What o'clock is it?"

"It is not yet ten, but please, she is greatly disturbed, maestro. She wrings her hands—so—and I think it is not well for that one to be in such a taking, not well for that which she carries beneath her heart."

He wasted no more time in questions. "My robe," he said crisply as he hurriedly got out of bed. He did not wait for the valet's help, but took the garment from his outstretched hands, donned it hastily, and strode into the parlor.

As Roberto had indicated, Mary was pacing up and down the room, clasping and unclasping her hands. "Peter," she moaned and ran to him. The face she turned up to him was drained of all color.

Quickly he placed an arm around her waist. "Mary, my dear, what's amiss?"

"It's T-Tiffany . . . she's gone," Mary wailed.

117

He grew cold remembering last night, remembering the cruelty that he had deemed a kindness, a kindness for them both. But Mary was still speaking and he must listen.

"She's been abducted, Tom has her."

"Tom?" he repeated. "Her brother?"

"Her stepbrother. He's none of ours, but there's much he knows; and he says if I were to tell a constable or—or the Bow Street Runners . . . but . . . but he knows I dare not. I—I must do as he requires, but Garnet's in Ireland—in a sense, it's his fault."

"His fault? How might that be, Mary?"

"If he had not been so hard on Tom the other night . . ."

"The other night? When?"

"On the night of your concert, Peter. Tom approached me. He needed money and Garnet threatened him with transportation. I did not want that. Tom's vindictive and I was frightened. But I—I never dreamed. Oh, Peter, I'd sell my jewels, but I dare not. They are Garnet's t-treasures—heirlooms. And H-Howard and Gibbs will not loan me half of what I need, and I must have the money by t-tonight, else T-Tiffany will suffer. He has threatened that she will s-suffer more each hour— after nine tonight, if he has not the money in his hands. Oh God, Peter, will you help me? You're wealthy and I—" She hid her face in her hands.

"Mary." He led her to a sofa. "Yes, I will help you, but you must calm yourself and tell me exactly what has happened, and when?"

"I barely understand what has happened," she said piteously. "M-Marie, her abigail, she has gone too. And since last night."

"Last night . . ." He frowned.

"Yes, but Peter, last night—all day yesterday she was ill. She could not go with Edmund and me to dinner at Lady Grey's. Yet one of the footmen told me he saw them both—Tiffany and Marie Duclos—leave the house in a *hired* carriage! Could she have been going to meet

Tom? But why would she when she hates him? He was always so cruel to her when she was younger. He and his father too."

"I remember," Peter said grimly. His mind was working rapidly. He might have known that Tiffany had slipped away from the house without telling anyone. He recalled her note: "I must see you—alone, dearest Peter, I have much to tell you." She had signed it "Your Tiffany." But she had *not* been *his* Tiffany. She was promised to Lord Wray, and precautions had to be taken before she acted impulsively, foolishly.

"Tom must have followed her here," he muttered, half to himself.

"Tom followed her . . . here? I do not understand."

He cursed himself for uttering his thoughts aloud, but there was no help for it. She had to know what had happened, even if it entailed explanations he was loathe to provide. "She was at the concert last night, Mary."

"At the concert?" she repeated blankly. "You saw her?"

"She came to see me," he explained.

"But why? And why—why should she pretend to be ill and . . ."

He chose his words with care. "Tiffany, for all that she is eighteen, must yet be very much of a child. She is full of romantic notions. Once she fancied herself in love with me. I discouraged her, of course. Last night, I was also discouraging and I fear I—wounded her. She left quickly, her abigail was with her."

Mary regarded him in amazement. "Surely, Peter, you are mistaken. She loves Edmund. She has told me so repeatedly. Of course she does. We'd not have forced her to wed him, and . . . and they are sewing on her g-gown and . . . oh God, God, but—She was at the theater, and with only her abigail to chaperone her! But she could not come out of l-love, Peter, though she was much moved by your music. She would have told *me*. She's always confided in me and . . . and Edmund is so eligible!"

"I am aware of that, Mary," he said dryly. "I am

sure it is a fine match. But as I have said, she is very young." He hesitated and then added meaningfully, "As you yourself know, my dear, very young girls can imagine they love those with whom they could not possibly be allied."

She flushed to the roots of her hair. "I . . . I do know. None better, none better. And Tom, you believe, followed her when she came from the theater?"

"Yes. There was a welter of carriages around the stage entrance. She might have paid her hackney to await her there, but it would more likely have been a short distance away. The streets back of the King's are narrow and winding. 'Twould be easy for Tom to overpower two young women and drag them into the shadows of some overhanging roof. And, of course, he might have had a confederate. He's been in prison. How much money does he want?"

"It—it's twenty-five thousand pounds, Peter."

"He shall have it."

She stared at him disbelievingly and tears started to her eyes again, "Oh, Peter, how may I ever thank you? I shall repay you some way, I shall—"

Impatiently he cut across her fragmented speech. "How is the money to be given him?"

"He says I am to place it in a portmanteau and take it to the Black Swan Inn, where I am to leave it for a man called Rake. I am to go alone. My movements will be observed there and back. If I am followed, if I come in company with anyone, if I attempt to inform the Runners, I—I shall never see my Tiffany alive again."

"And if you follow these directions, has he said he will bring her back?" Peter found that his lips were stiff.

"He has promised that if all goes well, he will bring her to my door at midnight."

"I will wait with you until midnight."

"Oh, Peter." She clasped her hands. "I . . . I do not know what to say. I am so . . . you are so good . . ."

"Enough, Mary," he said gently. "I only wish I might accompany you to the Swan."

"You cannot," she told him with another compulsive twist of her small hands. "But I am glad you have offered to wait with me—I will need your company."

"I shall make arrangements immediately for the money." He made a movement toward the door, looked at himself and laughed wryly. "You must wait for me, Mary. I shall be with you momentarily."

In the drawing room of the Cavendish mansion, blue flames ate at the crumbling remnants of a huge log. A high March wind had sprung up in the last hour and wailed dismally about the house. As the room grew cooler, Lady Mary, sitting tensely in a straight-backed chair, drew a soft rose-colored cashmere shawl about her shoulders.

Peter, who sat in a companion chair set directly across from her, asked, "Shall I add another log?"

"No, 'tis close to midnight." Her eyes, dark-circled and red-rimmed, were raised to the clock on the mantelpiece. " 'Tis but thirteen minutes hence. Are you chilled?"

"No," he replied, "I—" He paused as she raised her hand.

"Hssst, Peter, I heard a sound."

They both listened. Outside, reins rattled and there was the clip-clop of hooves. Mary broke the ensuing silence with a long sigh. " 'Twas but a passing carriage."

He nodded. " 'Tis not midnight yet." He bit down a sigh of his own. He was worried about Mary. She was so near her time. If Tom did not bring Tiffany back as was promised . . . He clenched his teeth, his anger rising, his nerves on edge. He wanted to pace the floor as Mary had done that morning. The chamber was built for pacing. It was long and wide, beautifully furnished—very like a state room and certainly fit for the reception of princes. The two of them were lost in it, but they had chosen to wait out the hours there because it was nearest the front door. There was a crack of sound. It echoed through that vast interior. A shower of sparks flying up the chimney indicated its origin—the fire had succeeded in devouring its way through the log.

"It's so late, suppose he does not—" Lady Mary began.

"He said midnight," Peter reminded her and wished his tones had not sounded so constricted.

"She . . . she must be so frightened," Lady Mary whispered. "He used to torment her, even when they were little. She went in fear of him, she would even cry out in her sleep."

A vagrant memory stirred at the back of his mind and vanished as he looked at Lady Mary. Contempt warred with pity. Her little girl had lived in terror, but she had done nothing about it. She was weak. She had been subservient to Sir Matthew, and she was subservient to Garnet Bland, the man who had threatened Tom. He could only be pleased Lord Cavendish was in Ireland—else he would have had the Bow Street Runners out in full force and Tiffany would have been lost. Meanwhile, what had happened to her? Was she being tormented by Tom? The memory beat once more at the back of his brain. He recalled her weeping in the night.

"Peter." Lady Mary scarcely articulated his name.

He tensed, hearing footfalls. Were they along the walk beyond the house? No, coming closer. A gate squeaked open, they were mounting the short flight of marble steps that led to the front door. The knocker rose and fell. He was into the hall in a trio of strides, with Lady Mary fluttering behind him uttering little moans.

He opened the door and the small, cloaked figure fell into his arms. Catching her up, he bore her into the drawing room.

"My love, T-Tiffany, my dearest, have they hurt you?" Lady Mary wailed as Peter laid his burden down on the sofa. The hood of her cape was low on her face. As he pushed it back, Mary screamed in horror.

Peter, staring at a dark face, black brows and a thin mouth which, even in her swoon, seemed disdainful, recognized the young woman who had accompanied Tiffany, the previous night. Her abigail!

" 'Tis Marie Duclos," Lady Mary corroborated on a

sob. "T-Tiffany, where is she, where is she? He promised he'd bring her back, what has he done with her?" She clutched Peter's arm.

"Have you hartshorn or can you burn some feathers, anything to rouse her?"

"Hartshorn," she repeated vaguely. "I do not know. The servants. I will ring . . ."

His patience was fast fraying. Mary's weakness and helplessness were wearing on nerves already badly strained. His was not a phlegmatic nature. The questions she was asking were rushing through his own mind together with terrifying answers. He said brusquely, "We sent the servants to bed, Mary, and for a very good reason. Surely you have a vinaigrette."

"A vinaigrette, yes, oh, I do. 'Tis in my chamber, I shall fetch it." She moved toward the door.

"Ah, *c'est noir, noir, noir,*" Marie moaned.

"She's awake." Lady Mary hurried back to the sofa. "Ask her—"

"Marie," Peter put his hand on the girl's arm.

"Aieeeee!" she shrieked, shrinking back. "Do not 'it me again."

He felt as if his blood had congealed in his veins, but he said gently, "No one will hurt you, my girl. You are safe."

"Ask her about Tiffany," Lady Mary prompted impatiently.

His own impatience arose to match hers. It was with an effort that he managed to say calmly, "She's in no condition to answer our questions, Mary. She must have a restorative. Brandy. Please fetch it."

Much to his relief, she made no objections and as she hurried out, the girl groaned, *"C'est terrible! Pourquoi? Ah, c'est noir* . . . so dark and so cold, I can see nothing."

His memory was piqued again. A dark room, a weeping child. Soon he would have the whole picture, but he could not dwell on it now. He bent over Marie. "Open your eyes, you will see that you are quite safe."

She moved restlessly, a hand stealing up to her chin. "It aches. Ah, *la pauvre petite*. Why did they 'urt 'er, the big woman beating 'er, so cruel . . ."

He put out a hand and took it back quickly. It was all he could do not to shake the girl into consciousness and demand that she tell him what had happened to Tiffany. He glanced about him. Where was Mary? Why was she taking such an unconscionably long time to fetch the brandy? Behind him the door creaked open and Lady Mary's breathy sighs were in his ear.

"Has she said anything else?"

"Please, the brandy," he said impatiently. "Pour a little into a glass."

"A glass?"

Looking around, he saw that she was clutching only the crystal decanter. Naturally she had forgotten the glass. "Give me the bottle, then," he rasped. More than ever, her helplessness annoyed him. Subduing an impulse to wrest it from her grasp, he grasped the decanter gently and as her hands fell away, he turned and brought it swiftly to Marie's lips.

She coughed and spluttered. "It burns."

"Tiffany," Lady Mary leaned over her. "Where is she, girl?"

"Gently, gently," Peter hissed. "You'll only confuse her."

"But—"

"Mary!" he said warningly.

"But she must *know!*" she cried.

"And must have time to recover her equilibrium."

"Ah, Monsieur Esdras." Marie blinked up at him.

He turned back to her quickly, meeting eyes that were no longer vague and confused. "Yes, you are better, then. Good."

"Ah, monsieur, I 'ave a message for milady."

"For me?" Mary cried. "Where is Tiffany, what have they done with her?"

The abigail's eyes were full of tears. "It is money they want. More, more, they 'ave told me. If there is not as much as 'twas presented before, all that is secret will be revealed in a broadside. *Tout le monde* will know. They 'ave said this. They 'ave said the money must be at the Black Swan by nine, and then the girl will be with you."

"Oh God, God, God." Lady Mary dropped to her knees, wailing.

Peter rose. "Can you walk, Marie?"

"Oui, monsieur."

"Come with me to the other side of the room. I have more questions."

"Peter, wait!" Lady Mary screamed. "Peter, oh God, Peter, I am being torn apart." Lying back, she pressed her hand against her stomach.

"Ah, milady." Marie slipped from the sofa and ran to Lady Mary's side. "Ah, Monsieur Esdras, 'er time is upon 'er. *Le docteur—vite, vite!*"

He knelt beside Lady Mary. He was neither ready nor willing to heed that frantic summons. It was possible that his cousin was only hysterical. It was Tiffany's plight that must come first—Tiffany, who, according to Marie, had been harshly treated by Tom or his accomplice. There was little sympathy in the gaze he leveled on Lady Mary, but on seeing her heaving body and the real agony in her eyes, he rose swiftly. His own fear, his own agony, even Tiffany's peril must be put aside for the time being.

"Do not move her," he cautioned the abigail. "Fetch pillows and a blanket. Make her as comfortable as you can. I shall find a doctor."

Dark, dark, dark, a chittering of rats in the walls, a chill hardness beneath her. She clutched her knees against her chest for warmth. Her clothes had been stripped from her and her thin silk shift was scant protection against the dank cold of the lower cellar—for she was back in that subterranean cavity that Tom had discovered all those years ago and where he had once left her screaming. She had dreamed about it, she remembered. She had dreamed about it often until the night Peter had come to comfort her, kiss her and banish her terrors.

He would not come now, there would be no awakening from the horror in which she dwelt. She had been in her prison for two days; she knew that because she had been fed four times. Terrible food, nameless messes of vegetables and scraps of meat together with dry crusts of bread and weak tea, but she had eaten it for she had been ravenously hungry, having had nothing on the day of the concert—the day of the disaster. She tensed and tears came into her eyes. Above the faint street noises that penetrated through the thin old walls, she heard the tuneless scraping of a street fiddler. She wished he would go away. Though it was a mere travesty of the music Peter had made, it brought him to mind as she had last seen him, standing in the dressing room, his arm around the female in green; the female who looked like the Sara of long ago, not the Sara who had glared at her in the corridor or whose hard punishing blows had fallen on her arms, her shoulders and her jaw so that one of her teeth felt loose beneath her probing tongue. She might have suffered worse had not Tom strode in to give Sara a box on the ear that sent her reeling.

She had cursed him loudly. "'Tis her fault, all that happened to me," she had railed. "And she'll pay for it."

" 'Twas your own fault what happened to you, doxy. 'Twas you who spread your legs for that stableboy," he had retorted with one of his boisterous laughs. "But no matter, you'll be well-recompensed for all you've suffered."

"I'll not be recompensed until she's in the river," Sara had cried. She had stepped to the couch where Tiffany was lying, still half-dazed from the effects of the ether that had rendered her unconscious, still aching from the cruel blows Sara had showered on her. Bending down, she had said, "Do you know what they'll do to you when they've fished out your corpse, wench? 'Twill be the dissecting rooms and your heart and liver pickled in brine!"

"Ah, *c'est terrible,* you do not talk in such a way to my mistress, *salope!*" Marie had cried in a faint quavering voice.

"No, you'll keep those pretty sentiments to yourself, my Sara," Tom had growled threateningly. Picking Tiffany up in his arms, he had carried her from the room, down a corridor, into another corridor, where he had been joined by someone carrying a lighted candle.

"Open the door," he had commanded.

She had heard the squeak of a rusty hinge and then they were descending a short flight of stairs, walking across an expanse of floor that echoed hollowly beneath his feet. Stopping, he said, "Now that door."

"Oi'd like to know 'ow ye found out about this 'un," a high cracked feminine voice had remarked crossly.

"Mrs. Bowes!" Tiffany had gasped.

"The same," Tom chuckled. "The princess remembers you, Mrs. Bowes. What do you think of that?"

"Oi don't like it by 'alf," the old woman grumbled. "If she's sent back—"

Tom's reply had sent chills coursing up and down her spine. They returned as she recalled it. He had only chuckled again.

"No fear of that Mrs. Bowes. Now open the door."

There had been an even louder, rustier screech of assaulted hinges and then he was carrying her down more stairs—the long flight of stairs she remembered from his terrifying prank all those years ago. Once again she had seen the small square chamber with its sagging wood and plaster wall. Tom had put her down and over her agonized protests, he had aided Mrs. Bowes to strip off her cloak and gown.

He had said incomprehensibly, " 'Tis a pity we may not keep the cloak, 'twould fetch fine price. But the gown must suffice. Easy with her stockings, they are silk," he had added, as the old woman pulled off her shoes.

She had been careful with the hose, exclaiming over their fineness. "None but the best for 'er," she had muttered vindictively, "I'll get a length o' rope'n ye may bind 'er."

"That's not needed. How would she get out through a locked door and in her shift?" he had laughed.

"But—"

127

"Get along with you, Mrs. Bowes," he had ordered. "And leave me the candle. I'll have a word with Taffy, here."

Shudder after shudder wracked her as she recalled Tom coming to stand beside her, holding Mrs. Bowes's candle in one hand and a small pistol in the other. "Just in case you've a mind to make a dash for it," he had said, showing it to her.

Even without the weapon pointing at her, she could not have moved—she was frozen with horror. The flickering flame of the candle had traced strange diagonal lines on his cheeks and thrown the middle part of his face into darkness; there was an eerie glow to his red brown eyes and a metallic cast to his bright hair. In the mocking tone she knew so well, he had said, "And does not our princess care for her realm?"

Once she had screamed and wept and begged him not to leave her here. But even knowing that such was to be her fate once more, she had downed the cries of fear forming in her throat and said coldly, "Why have you brought me to this place?"

"Ask the fair Cyprian who calls herself Lady Cavendish!" he had replied. "But that is impossible, is it not? Indeed, my poor Taffy, I very much fear you will never set eyes upon your Lady Mother again. So I will explain why you are briefly ensconced in Mrs. Bowes's lodgings. Because I need money, but since your stepfather has threatened me with transportation and since I do not fancy another stint in prison—especially if it be in New South Wales—I am holding you for ransom. Your mama will pay as she has before—and there'll be others who'll pay, too. You need not fear that I shall honor Sara's wishes. 'Tis not the river for you, my love. You've grown a pretty little body and a lovely little face, and there's many an abbess'll bid high for a nun can claim the Prince Regent for a father. There's always a high premium on the blood royal, no matter from which side of the blanket 'tis poured."

"I do not understand you."

"I am sure you do not. But it might please you to know, my dearest Taffy, that 'twas the Regent begot you on the loins of our Mary, when she was visiting her sister Susanna, who was maid of honor to his mama, the Queen. That caused a great to-do in certain circles, but it died down when the sinning sister disappeared. 'Twas rumored she was dead, but actually, well fortified with the Regent's gold, she'd gone to a certain abbey to drop her bastard. So you can see 'twas a Walesman if not a Welshman that scattered the seeds from which you took root."

" 'Tis not true."

"I think that if you were to see the likeness of a certain loose lady named Sophia Dorothea, who was the ancestress of our Regent, you'd find that you had some features in common. Namely, the tip-tilted eyes and the mouth. I myself was inclined to think it all a fabrication when my father told me about it. And damned angry about it he was, finding that the fair and wealthy widow he'd wed was not a widow after all. It caused quite a breech between him and the Regent. At any rate, 'twas he showed me a miniature of Sophia Dorothea. It still remains in my possession and I shall circulate it to any prospective customers for your hand—if not your heart. Though I fear I must tell you that your marriage prospects have become very dim. Still, who knows? You may, like our Sara, find life as a whore much to your liking. I am told that your great, etc. grandmother Sophia Dorothea greatly enjoyed the pleasures of concupiscence until her lover was murdered and she imprisoned. That fate, at least, will not befall you, my Taffy."

"It's not true!" she had cried again.

He had only laughed and gone, leaving her in darkness with the thoughts that yet tormented her, that would never cease to torment her. "It's not true, not true," she whispered. It could not be true. Her mother and the Prince . . . Yet there had been his unusual kindness to her.

From the very first, he had been kind, but he had

also been kind to other people. He was known to be especially partial to the young. Lord Cavendish had commented on the pleasure he took in the company of Mrs. Fitzherbert's young daughter, whom he still entertained at Carlton house, though her mother had long been out of favor. Yet, he had known that girl for years. After all, she had lived in the house he had shared with her mother in Brighton.

Her own father had been Irish, an Irish officer. She frowned, remembering how seldom Lady Mary had mentioned him. It occurred to her that all her life, she had had trouble believing in his existence. But he had died before she had been born. Her mind veered away from him to Lady Mary's family. It had seemed to consist only of two cousins—Ellen and Anne. Kind Ellen. Censorious Anne, who had always seemed to look down her nose at Lady Mary. Her mother had never mentioned her own parents, nor had she ever had much to confide about her childhood and her early youth, save to say that a portion of it had been spent at the abbey with Ellen and her widower father.

Then there had been that strange little reference to the very great debt she owed her Cousin Ellen. Had that debt been incurred by her providing a haven for a young woman expecting an illegitimate child?

"She fainted," Tiffany murmured and was momentarily surprised. The thought had flitted into her mind and out again. She called it back, pondering it reluctantly. Her mother had fainted—when? Months ago in the ballroom at Carlton house. The seizure had been attributed to her condition. Yet, Tiffany remembered, she had been so disturbed that evening that she had been reluctant to go to the ball. She had also always been loathe to visit the abbey, even while praising Cousin Ellen's great kindness to her in the past.

Ellen and Peter. Did Peter know of her heritage, her base birth? Was that why he wanted nothing to do with her? No, it was his music that kept them apart. She could not believe Tom. He was lying. If she could see her mother and ask her . . . but she would never see her again. She shuddered. Tom had not explained what an abbess was. He knew he had no need to. His step-sister had also resided in Sir Matthew's house, had heard his jeering references to abbesses and nunneries. An abbess kept a brothel, a nun was a whore. But she would not be a whore. Better the river and the dissecting knives!

She tensed. She had heard a sound outside her door. Mrs. Bowes must be coming to feed her. It had been hours since she had last eaten.

Soon the door would be unlocked, and the old woman would set down the candle. Cocking the pistol Tom must have provided, she would croak, "'Ere's yer grub." Tiffany, blinking against the light, would make her way across the floor and up the narrow steps to take the food. Once she had the plate in her hands and had returned to her pile of rags, the old woman would slam the door, leaving her in Stygian darkness.

In the morning, the routine differed only slightly. Tom would hold the pistol, while the old woman, candle in hand, would take out the slop jars and give her a pitcher of fresh water.

She wondered how much longer she would remain in the room. But terrible as her incarceration was, the leaving of her prison would be even worse. For the way out must lead to shame, disgrace and death. As always, she stiffened as she heard the jingle of keys. The door creaked open and Tiffany, again half blinded by the candleflame, gasped in horror. Her fears had been realized! It was not Mrs. Bowes, who stood there, nor was it Tom. The man framed in the aperture was taller, thinner. The procurer from the brothel? Trembling, she huddled down among her rags.

"Tiffany?" The voice was uncertain. "Are you there? I cannot see you."

Her voice was the merest whisper. "You . . . no, I must be dreaming. Or I have gone mad! It . . . it cannot be Peter."

"Thank God, thank God," he said brokenly. "Are you bound? I have a knife." He started down the steps.

"No," she croaked. "Do not come down, the steps

are steep and narrow, you might lose your footing. I can walk. How did you find me?"

"Do not stop to question me. Hurry."

She felt weak, light-headed with shock. But she was able to clamber up the steps and in a moment she was beside Peter. He put an arm around her, holding her tightly while he shone the candle into her face. In that same flame, she saw that he was dressed in old ragged clothing, his shirt gaping open on his bare chest. More questions sprung to her lips, but at that moment, the candleflame quivered in a sudden rush of air. Glancing upward, she saw that a door ahead of them had been flung open.

"Mrs. Bowes! Mrs. Bowes, are you down there?" an irate voice called.

"Tom," she breathed.

Pulling her to one side, Peter blew out his candle.

The door slammed against the wall and Tom, carrying a small lantern, entered. "Mrs. Bowes, you old crone, where the hell are you? What'd you do with the money?" he growled. Seeing that the door to the second cellar was open, he moved forward hastily, peering down the steps and at that moment, Peter leaped toward him, but quick as his movement was, Tom turned to confront him. "You —who're you?"

Hands outstretched, he lunged at Peter, closing with him and bearing him to the floor, while the lantern, spinning out of his grasp, crashed against the wall.

Tiffany watched in horror as the two men grappled together silently. She looked about her, hoping to find a stick. If she could strike Tom—but it was too dark. She coughed and coughed again. There was smoke seeping into her nostrils. *Smoke!* She looked around her and cried out in fright. Small tongues of flame were leaping from what appeared to be a bundle of old rags, similar to those upon which she had lain. The lantern must have broken and ignited them! Even as she watched, the flames grew brighter, feeding on other objects strewn about the dirty floor.

132

She ran toward the two men. "Fire, fire!" she screamed.

They did not seem to hear her. Tom was dealing punishing blows to Peter. But he, slimmer and more agile, was striking back and appeared to be holding his own. But the fire was spreading, its flames leaping high and the room filling with choking smoke. Coughing, Tom loosened his grip and staggered to his feet, backing away from the encroaching blaze as Peter also got to his feet.

Rushing to him, Tiffany seized his hand. "Come, come quickly," she urged, then stopped, arrested by a loud yell and a series of thuds.

"There." Peter pointed to the door. "He must have fallen down the stairs." He hurried toward the opening.

"You cannot go after him," she screamed.

"I cannot leave him there. Go into the hall, go." He gave her a little push and ducked down into the doorway.

"Peter!" She dashed after him. "Come back, come back." Unmindful of the nearing flames, she stared down into the fire-illumined cavity below and then Peter was hurrying up the steps again.

"I told you to go," he cried hoarsely. Seizing her hand, he dragged her across the room and into the corridor. "The old woman," he groaned. "We left her here." He pointed to a door that Tiffany knew led into a large closet. Wrenching it open, he hurried inside, emerging with the trussed and gagged form of Mrs. Bowes over his shoulder. She was writhing and uttering strangled sounds, but he grasped her firmly, looking about in confusion, coughing as the smoke billowed around them. "How can we get out?"

Prodded by memory, she could say, "I know the way. Come." She moved into a passage and in a few moments, she had led him out through the front door and into the street.

A crowd was already gathering and Peter, still carrying Mrs. Bowes, said to Tiffany, "Keep fast hold of my other arm, we must get to my carriage."

As she obeyed, he started to force his way through the throngs when a small, black-clad man rushed up to them. Tiffany recognized his valet.

"Maestro, maestro," he gasped. *"Sono felice—"*

"Basta, basta!" Peter muttered. Setting his writhing burden down, he pointed to Tiffany, uttering directions in Italian.

"Si, si, maestro." The little man smiled and nodded. Taking off his jacket, he handed it to Peter, who put it about Tiffany. She felt herself grow warm with embarrassment; she had forgotten she was wearing only her shift.

"Come, my dear." Peter put his arm around her while Roberto easily lifted Mrs. Bowes, hurrying on ahead of them. As they edged through the crowds, Tiffany, looking back, saw that the flames were visible through the windows. Other figures were running from the house. Then a hoarse scream was in her ears as a woman pushed her way past those standing on the sidewalk. She dashed toward the open door but was pulled back by a man standing near her. She wailed and gesticulated. As the lurid glow from the burning house fell on her face, Tiffany recognized Sara!

"Come." Peter's voice was edged with impatience.

"But that—" She paused as Sara, still screaming, wrested herself from the arms of the man holding her and fled into the house.

"Peter." Tiffany stopped short.

He lifted her in his arms. "Child, I pray you—"

"Sara, Sara!" she screamed, her own anguished cry echoed by the horrified bystanders as the flames rose high in the doorway.

"Sara? What about her?" Peter had also halted.

Sobbing, Tiffany clung to him. "She ran into the house, she must be—oh, Peter."

He paled but shook his head. "We can do nothing, the wood's old and dry, it—" His voice broke and holding her close against him, he strode on across the street toward a battered old carriage, drawn by a spavined nag. Incongruously, Roberto was holding its reins.

Giving him some instructions, Peter helped Tiffany inside and climbing in after her, he gathered her into his arms once more, stroking her hair gently. Caught between horror at what she had witnessed and a joy she could not suppress, she hid her tearful face against his chest.

Eight

A little more than two hours after her dramatic rescue, Tiffany, revived by a long, lovely bath and temporarily enveloped in one of Peter's nightshirts, lay in his large four-poster, looking expectantly at the bedroom door. According to Roberto, who had come to take away the copper bathtub, his master had gone to procure some garments for her—from his manager's wife. Yet, certainly he had been gone a very long time. She moved restlessly, longing for him to return.

She was feeling very happy, for the shock of Sara's terrible death had largely passed. She could not grieve overlong for one who had not only beaten her but had urged Tom to drown her in the Thames! It was also difficult to mourn the passing of Tom, dead of a broken neck, in that same cellar where he had imprisoned her. Nor could she expend any sympathy on Mrs. Bowes, remanded to the care of the constable and destined either for Newgate or New South Wales. Roberto had told her that secreted in the old woman's apron pocket had been a great deal of the money that Tom had demanded as ransom and which Peter had provided. It must have been that same money that had brought Sara back into the burning house. She shuddered, dismissing that reprehensible trio from her mind. There were other far more pleasant subjects that must occupy it now.

Incredibly, she had a new little sister; even more incredibly, given the circumstances attendant upon the birth, mother and child were in good health. Though certainly this news had delighted her, she was not thinking about her mother or her sibling. She was concentrating upon Peter and her rescue. How had he managed it? No, that was not the main question! How had he discovered her whereabouts?

He could not have been in communication with either Tom or Sara. Mrs. Bowes could not have dropped that flea in his ear. It was very mysterious, it was even magical. Could he have consulted a seer? Her common sense told her that he would not. Yet, how else might he have found her? She concentrated on the door, willing him to enter, and at that moment it swung open and he was there. More magic!

She drew a deep breath, staring at him in wonder, thinking that never had she seen him look more handsome. He was wearing a gray coat, just a little darker than his eyes. His face was beautiful with its aquiline features, its look that was not wholly English yet not wholly foreign, either. No man she had ever known had so slim or well-proportioned a figure, or legs that looked better in tight gray trousers, clipped under his boots; and surely no one seeing his intricate cravat and the pristine whiteness of his linen would have guessed that only two hours earlier, he had been dirty, soot-streaked and ragged. Those rags must be explained, too, as well as the battered equipage in which he had brought her to his lodgings. Then, as he came within range of the light glowing in the candelabra near the bed, she noticed a cut on his cheek and a dark swelling around one eye.

"Oh," she mourned, "your poor eye!"

A smile was reflected in both eyes as he came

nearer. " 'Tis nothing." His smile faded to be replaced by an anxious expression. "You've suffered far more than I. Your arms, your jaw . . ."

"Please, I beg you'll not think on it." She gave him a loving little smile. "It is less than nothing." Reaching out, she caught his hand. "Sit down, I beg you and have pity on my ignorance. How ever did you find me?"

The fingers on the hand she held worked themselves free and fastened around her hand in turn, giving it a loving little squeeze. A mischievous smile tugged at the corners of his mouth. " 'Twas you gave me the direction."

"I!"

"Years ago," he continued, "you had a dream and cried out during the night. I expect you'd not remember."

"I do remember. I remember every moment that I have spent with you, but how did you happen to recall anything so trivial."

" 'Twas not trivial." He sat down on the edge of the bed. "You were terrified, poor child. You told me all about a cellar beneath a cellar, a dark place in that lodging house, and Tom leaving you there. Various things your mother said last night jogged my memory. I thought 'twas possible he might have hidden you there. It seemed a very likely place for him to use. I admit that I was not entirely hopeful, but nothing was hopeful once they'd played that cruel trick and left Marie in your place. I had fears that if I did not find you, you might be lost to me forever."

"Yes. They talked of selling me to a brothel."

He went white. "Damn them, damn them, if I'd known that!" He smote the bed with his clenched fist.

"My dear, could they have suffered more if you had known?"

His hand slowly unclenched. "No, you're right. The price has been paid." He fell silent, gazing at the floor.

"My dearest," she prompted. "How did you get into the house and why were you wearing such rags?"

He lifted his eyes and now there was a hint of

laughter reflected in their gray depths. "Those rags were the garb of a street musician."

"Oh, I heard a violin, but 'twas a terrible noise. It could not have been you."

"I should like to blame the instrument but 'twas both of us. It *was* terrible, was it not?" he said with some satisfaction. "I ranged up and down that street begging for coins all the day, while those who heard me either cursed or begged me to take myself off. I earned no money, but I gained the gold I sought when I spotted your late stepbrother coming out of the house!"

"How did you know him?"

"I saw him as a child. He'd not changed so much. There was that hair."

"That hair, yes." She grimaced. "But how did you get into the house?"

He looked at her solemnly. "I attribute that to fate and Roberto. He was waiting in the carriage while I wandered the streets."

"That carriage, that horse!" she laughed.

"Yes, they were purchased from an old-clothes dealer. I thought they must look less conspicuous in that enclave."

"I did not mean to interrupt, tell me the rest," she said eagerly.

"Well, near sunset when I deemed it safe, I instructed Roberto to meet me in the alley back of the house. We approached it from two different directions and met fate in the person of Mrs. Bowes, returning from the market. I recognized her as the old woman who'd stood in the door of the lodging house when I came to fetch you. I signaled to Roberto and he came to twist her arms behind her back. I had a knife and I confronted her with it. On the chance that she was as cowardly as most bullies are, I put it to her throat and told her I would slit it from ear to ear if she did not tell me where you were. She tried to scream, but Roberto clapped his hand across her mouth and I gave her the point of the knife."

"Peter!" Tiffany gasped.

"The smallest prick, my love. A flea bite. But 'twas

enough. She did not scream when Roberto removed his hand. She talked. And at another fleabite or perhaps 'twas a bee sting, she produced the keys, and Roberto some twine with which he bound her. We carried her into the house and put her in that closet. Then I bade him go back to the carriage. That was unwise, but I'd banked on Tom's not returning."

"Unwise? It was madness. You could have been killed," she breathed.

"But I was not."

"Oh God, it passes all understanding. You, with a knife—who are so gentle—you fighting with Tom."

"I had great incentive," he said grimly. "I had incentive enough to strangle him with these two hands."

She seized his hands, pressing them to her lips. "Oh, Peter, Peter, Peter, I love you so much. Can you say now that you do not love me, do not want me?"

"No." He was breathing hard. "I—I cannot say that, but you are promised."

"Promised. I shall be unpromised. I do not care for him. I never, never have. It was only that I thought you—your letter. It hurt me so dreadfully. How could you have been so cruel?"

"I thought it a kindness."

"I wanted to die, and it was not kind. You were not thinking of me but your music. Is it still your music that stands between us? Do you love it more than me? But I'll not interfere with it. I only want to be with you."

He put his arms around her, holding her against him. "I do not love anything more than you, Tiffany, but—"

"Then there can be no buts, no more procrastination."

"My dear child—"

"I am not a child. Oh, why do you hesitate? If you love me, I am yours. I have been yours ever since I first saw you!" Wrenching herself from his grasp, she slipped from the bed, and facing him, she tore at the two sides of the nightshirt, baring her breasts. "Take me. Take me here on this bed, take me now and keep me the whole night, a thousand nights if you will. If you do not want marriage, let me be your whore!"

"Tiffany!" Leaping from the bed, he grasped her shoulders. "You do not know what you are saying!"

"I do, I do," she cried. "I am not ignorant of the world. I know that that woman, that golden woman in your dressing room is your mistress. I know that—"

He caught her to him, slipping his hand over her mouth. "You know nothing," he retorted hotly. "I have no mistress. She is the wife of my manager. I beg you will cease this foolish wild talk! If I am to marry you, I shall do it honorably. I shall offer for you as is right and proper. I shall—"

"Oh, Peter," she squeaked joyfully, "do you mean it?"

"Yes, I mean it." Sternly he added, "Cover yourself!"

She blushed and pulled the torn shirt together. "It was wrong of me," she said in a small voice, "but I wanted to make a point."

An unwilling smile curled his lips. "You succeeded."

"Will you . . . really offer for me?"

"Yes."

"Tonight?"

"Saturday afternoon."

"That's two days away."

"Your mother's had a baby."

"You said she was in good health."

"No matter, we must wait. And now, I have procured clothing for you and I want you to dress. I am taking you home."

She felt an unexplainable stab of fear. "No, I want to stay here."

"You will do as I say, or I'll not wed you."

She laughed at that, but she was still uneasy. "I do not want to leave you."

"Are you afraid I shall change my mind?" He was smiling at her tenderly, so tenderly!

"No . . . only—"

"Tiffany," he said almost solemnly, "when I tried to

turn you away, I thought it was for your own good, but when I was faced with the thought of your peril, I felt as though my heart had been torn from my body. No living being can exist without a heart and you are mine. If you'd not spoken, I—well, I was primed for it."

"Oh, Peter." She held out her arms.

He embraced her. His kiss was gentle, then passionate as he strained her against him. Releasing her, he said softly, "You can be sure of me, my own darling. Do you believe me now?"

"Yes." She could say no more. She dared not tell him that she was still strangely afraid. It would not have made sense to him, nor did it make sense to her. Yet she was.

Tiffany, clad in the blue she knew to be Peter's favorite color—at least for her—stood at her window. His post chaise was drawing to a stop in front of the house. She breathed a long sigh of relief, wishing that she might run down to him, but it had been her mother's gentle but firm request that she remain in her room until the interview was at an end. It was difficult to accede to that stipulation. She had not seen him for three days!

Her mother had been sleeping when Tiffany returned; she had awakened the following morning to a joyful reunion with her daughter. Afterward, she had listened with surprise but also with great sympathy to Tiffany's sentiments concerning Peter. Amazingly, she had offered no argument. She had only begged that his offer be postponed until Monday.

Tiffany's heart had plummeted. "I love him, Mama," she had said steadily. "I shall never love anyone else. I will write to Edmund immediately."

"No." Lady Mary had looked alarmed. "I pray you will not, else you will make me out a liar, child. I—I did not want to worry him, so I told him . . . I told everyone that you were abed with a virulent fever and under doctor's care. Let it stand at that. As for Peter, I shall be glad to hear him, my love, but you must remember that I tire easily. The dearest baby, do you not agree? But I am no longer young and I have yet to find a wet nurse. If only dear Garnet were here! But he is not and so much has descended upon my shoulders. Please, I beg you, forebear, and let me send a note to Peter. He will understand. He is always so understanding." She had added tenderly, "Do not glare at me, my dearest. I promise you that I shall let nothing keep me from seeing him on Monday. Such a little time will not matter, not when the two of you have your whole lives ahead of you. If you distrust me, you may read what I write."

Of course she had not done that, but she wished she might have seen Peter during the last two days. If Marie had been herself, Tiffany would have sent her to his lodgings with a note begging that he meet her in the Square, but Marie was still prostrate from her experience, and though Tiffany was loathe to admit it, she herself was suffering a reaction from her own ordeal. She had spent a great deal of her time sleeping, which was just as well, for her waking hours had passed with a painful slowness. Yet, they had passed, and he was here, stepping down from the post chaise, looking marvelously handsome in his many-caped coat and tall beaver hat. She wished that he would look up at her windows—but he did not. She wished too that she might linger in the hall outside the drawing room door, but her mother had forbidden it.

"You must stay in your chamber until I send for you, my love. No matter what your feelings, 'tis well to abide by the proprieties. I am sure Peter would agree with me."

"Damn the proprieties!" she muttered. She had half a mind to go downstairs anyhow, but, unfortunately, she was positive that Peter would agree with her mother. With a long-suffering look at the clock, she settled down in a chair and tried to read another chapter of *Emma*, even though she was quite out of sympathy with its prosy heroine!

Lady Mary lay on the chaise longue and Peter, entering, thought she looked very beautiful and very much at peace with the world, not unlike a Rafael Madonna he had seen in Florence.

As he bent over her hand, she regarded him with a soft smile. "Peter, how can I ever thank you?" she began. He listened courteously, albeit impatiently, to her words of gratitude and praise for his daring, his bravery. Yet, oddly, throughout her discourse, he was conscious of a growing foreboding. Was she a shade too effusive? Were not her hands too restless and her gaze oddly evasive? Or was he imagining it? He could, he knew, dismiss those observations as a form of nervous strain. He was tense and on edge. Though he knew Mary well, had known her all of his life and had not always respected or admired her, he had to remember that he was applying for the hand of her daughter.

How different they were, he mused. If Mary had been subjected to the pain, the threats and all the terrors that had befallen Tiffany in Mrs. Bowes's cellar, she would have been reduced to gibbering idiocy by the time he had come for her. Yet Tiffany had never once lost her head. She rarely indulged in tears, though once in a garden . . .

"Peter."

He started slightly, coming out of his ruminations to find Mary regarding him gravely. He felt an odd throb in his chest. "Yes, Mary."

"My dear, my daughter tells me that you are here to offer for her."

"Yes, that is true, I—"

She held up her hand. "Peter, before you say anything else, let me beg you to reconsider. Let me beg you not to be so very thoughtless."

"Thoughtless?"

She studied her small, beringed hands. "I know you will resent my use of that word. I am sure you are fond of Tiffany."

"I am not fond of her, Mary. I love her."

"Please, Peter, I beg you will heed me. Do sit here." She indicated a chair drawn up to her chaise longue.

145

"I think I should prefer to stand."

"As you choose, but please, I beg your indulgence. Let me have my say and then I shall hear you. You say you love her, and it is because of that that I beg you to be more understanding. Tiffany is very young, very emotional, very childish. Whereas you, who are twelve years her senior, are a mature man, a famous man. Yet I fear you might be deluding yourself. Did you not tell me that she cherished a romantic fancy for you that you had tried to discourage?"

"I did but I find——"

"Peter, you may say that you find you were mistaken, that her love is real, but I think you are wrong. Tiffany *is* in the clouds. She's up in her room, holding her breath, I am sure, awaiting my summons so that she can come down and throw herself into your arms. But my dear, four months ago, she was in just such a state over Edmund. Yes, equally excited—even ecstatic! She loved him, she loves you. She is in love with love!

"And, of course, it was such a romantic rescue. She believes she owes you her life. Well, I agree with that, and she is determined to make you a present of it, even though her marriage is no more than three months away and Edmund deeply in love with her—as she was with him and impatiently counting the days until they could be wed. You should have heard her!" She sighed and added, "Edmund is such an eligible young man."

"Which I am not?" he said harshly.

"Which you are not, my dear," she said regretfully, "though that is not your fault. Yet society, which flocks to hear you play, does not welcome one of your profession, one of your race to its bosom. Oh, I know you are half a Clive, but your father . . ."

He drew himself up. "I am very proud of my father, Mary."

"That does you great credit," she said smoothly, "yet you must agree that his is a heritage that is looked upon with scant favor here in England. I think such an attitude is ridiculous. But I, alas, am in the minority, and though I am not ambitious for my daughter, I see how

146

she is welcomed in the great houses to which she now has access. She is warmly received, and she has been very happy these last four months—again with Edmund. They are, you must agree, a beautiful young couple and much has been made over them. If she marries you, what will be her fate? She will be accepted by a certain group of people—musicians and their ilk—but so many doors will be shut against her.

"She will, I have no doubt, swear she does not care. That is not true, Peter. She does care. And she could be a great hostess. Edmund is politically ambitious. With her at his side, he might become a member of the Cabinet. If, on the other hand, she casts her lot with you, she will be a wanderer like yourself. Only, unlike you, she will not have the solace of a career. You love it and have no intention of relinquishing it for her, I am sure, so there will be times when you are parted by it, times when she'll be desperately lonely and unhappy. She will try to conceal her unhappiness, but she will not be totally successful and you will be made unhappy. Surely that is not the sort of atmosphere in which you will play your best. Your only alternative will be to send her to the abbey—to Ellen, where she will be equally lonely as your mother is lonely, ignored by the community in which she grew up. Because even though your father's dead, no one can forget the mistake she made, nor forgive the fact that she married some one—so very unacceptable."

"It might surprise you to know, Mary, that my mother chooses to live alone because she reveres my father's memory, and cannot forgive her so-called friends for the attitude they adopted long ago." Peter was controlling himself with an effort, but there was a tinge of fury as he added, "My mother has had many invitations. It is her choice that she does not accept them. It is she who cannot forgive or forget."

"She would not be placed in such a position if it were not for her marriage."

"She loved my father with all her being."

"I know, but you were the sufferer, were you not?"

"I?"

"Remember your childhood at the abbey, Peter. You were very lonely, you were taunted by the village boys. They cried 'Jew, Jew, Jew.'"

He raised his hand. "I—"

"Oh, I know you stood up to them, and I know that once you were cruelly beaten for it by some ruffians. I expect you've forgotten, but I have not. I was there. I remember Ellen's agony. If you marry Tiffany, what will be the fate of your children. They'll share your ostracism. They'll be like you—neither one nor the other. Is it right to take advantage of my daughter's delusion and—"

"Delusion?"

She shook her head. "My dear, have you not been listening. You say she loves you. I tell you that she has always confided in me, and the only words of love I have ever heard her utter concerned Edmund—until she returned from the horror that Tom thrust upon her. Think about that. Think about all that I have said and ask yourself if it were not better that you found someone of your own kind . . ."

She continued speaking, but he was no longer listening. He was remembering his mother's words. She had mentioned Tiffany's letters. They had been, she had told him, full of praise for Edmund. "She seems ecstatically happy," Ellen had said. And Mary had made sense. There was a deep and virulent prejudice against his father's people—against his people. He winced as he remembered Sara's hurtful words all those years ago, and Sara's screaming in his dressing room not a week since. She spoke for most of the insular English and much as he hated that attitude, it was there.

It particularly grated on him that the father whom he had adored must have suffered it, too. He had been a fine man, a fine musician, a loving parent, a loving husband, and he had made his mother very happy. She had cared nothing for the prejudice.

"'Thy people will be my people and thy Gods my Gods,'" was a favorite phrase of hers. Was Tiffany's love strong enough to surmount these obstacles? Might she not

148

make mountains out of what he believed to be the merest of molehills?

It was true, too, that he had his music. It was true that he would not, could not give it up. And there was Mary, weak, selfish and self-deluding. He could see nothing of Mary in Tiffany, but might she not have been infected by some of her mother's attitudes? How well did he know her? Was she really deluding herself? Was she lost in a romantic fantasy? Was he deluding himself? He remembered her plea that he take her as his whore— certainly that was a childish gesture!

His heart had become a leaden weight in his breast, but he was not going to spend the rest of his life cosseting an unhappy little girl who, in common with her mother, would never grow up. Nor was he going to try and please her by denying that he was proud of his heritage, proud of the father he had loved—no, not even for Tiffany.

"Peter," Mary said nervously, "I pray you—"

He raised his hand. "You need offer up no more prayers, Mary," he told her contemptuously. "I am glad to see you looking so well. Pray tell Tiffany that I came to inquire after her health only."

"I cannot tell her that."

"No doubt you will think of something that will suffice."

"You have no more to say to her?"

"Only farewell." He bent over her hand and hurriedly left the room, not waiting for the butler to usher him out.

Tiffany, standing at the balustrade in the upper hall, saw him striding toward the front door. "Peter," she called, but she was answered only by the closing of that same door. Incredulously, she stared down and then, running back to her windows, she was in time to see him climb into the post chaise and give an order to his coachman. The man cracked his whip and the vehicle was on its way.

"Peter!" She ran down the stairs and into the drawing room where Lady Mary still lay on the chaise longue

—a faint, satisfied smile on her lips. The expression vanished as Tiffany confronted her, crying, "Why did he go?"

"My dear, my nerves," her mother protested.

"Damn your nerves! Did he not offer for me as he had promised?"

"My poor child, I knew you must be mistaken. Peter is an honorable man and knowing you betrothed—"

Tiffany stamped her foot. "He came here to offer for me, I tell you!"

"My dear, you are sadly mistaken. He came here to inquire after my health and yours."

"You're lying!"

"Tiffany, how dare you speak to me that way? Go to your chamber at once!"

"I shall go nowhere until you tell me the truth!"

"I have told you the truth. He did not offer for you! That is the truth!"

"Then, what did you tell him? How did you discourage him from offering for me?"

"My dear, calm yourself."

"I am perfectly calm. What did you say to him, Mother? He was here quite a while. He did not spend all that time in inquiring after my health or yours."

Lady Mary gave a small sob. "I—I do not like your t-tone, Tiffany. It is very hard for a mother—"

"Do not weep," Tiffany commanded harshly. "You'll only make your eyes red, your tears will have no other effect. I ask you once more, Mother, *what did you say to Peter?*"

Lady Mary quailed. She had never seen her daughter look so ferocious. She was actually afraid of her. "I said only what I happen to know is the truth. You have had a terrible experience, child. You are not thinking straight. You must sort out your emotions. You are betrothed to a fine young man of excellent family. Your position in life is assured. You cannot exchange these prospects for life with a man who by blood and profession will never be accepted into the society into which you have been born."

"I see." Tiffany looked at her with a contempt

mixed with horror. "You told him that, I expect. You taxed him with his Jewish blood. I have no doubt of that, either. How could you be so cruel to a man who is worth all of anyone we know? Including your precious husband —including Edmund."

"I cannot let you speak that way. I know you are grateful to him."

"Grateful . . . I love him."

"My dear, your position."

"I pray you'll stop mentioning my position. I do not care about position, I want only Peter."

"That is not true. Of course you care. You must, though you'll not admit it. You are one of us, Tiffany, and—and the Prince has taken an interest in you. Does that mean nothing to you?"

Tiffany was silent a moment. "Yes," she said finally, "that does mean something to me, Mother."

"Ah," Lady Mary breathed. "You are beginning to see reason. I thought you must."

"The Prince is very fond of me, is he not?"

"Very fond, child."

"And this puts me above Peter?"

"I did not say that it puts you above or below," Lady Mary said patiently. "I only said that you are destined to tread a path different from his, and you have given your word to Edmund."

"I see. I am pleased that you have admitted that I am not above Peter. Because father or no father, he, at least, is legitimate."

Lady Mary sat bolt upright. "What do you mean by that?"

"I am sure you know what is meant by 'legitimate,' Mama. It explains a great deal to me—including your marriage to Sir Matthew Prine as well as his treatment of your bastard daughter."

"T-T-Tiffany," Lady Mary gasped. "How did you —" She broke off. "I mean, who was it told you such arrant nonsense? Your father was—"

"The Prince of Wales, Mama? That is what Tom said."

"And you believed him?"

"No," Tiffany said slowly. "It sounded plausible, but I was not sure I believed him. However, I believe you. I can see it in your eyes. And if I needed any further corroboration, I could cite your extreme nervousness on the night we went to Carlton House for the first time, as well as your fainting."

"I was expecting a child!"

"And never fainted again. 'Twas an amazingly untroubled and healthy pregnancy. The doctor was delighted. He exclaimed on it often. I am pleased, too, Mama. I hope you have many more children. But as for your ambitions concerning me, I suggest you direct them toward my legitimate sister." Turning on her heel, she moved swiftly toward the door.

"Tiffany, Tiffany, come back!" Lady Mary cried.

She did not heed that anguished plea. Running up the stairs, she hurried into her chamber, and pulling a reticule from her drawer, she emptied the contents of her jewelry case into it, and taking her cape from its hook on the door, she dashed down the stairs and out the front door.

Informed by an impassive butler that a lady had called to see him, Lord Ballard frowned. "You know that I am never at home to ladies of that ilk, Oakes," he said coldly.

"It is Miss Prine who has asked for you, my lord."

"Miss Prine," Edmund exclaimed. With a face which rivaled that of his butler in impassiveness, he said, "Then, of course you must admit her, though I need not explain, I am sure, that you did not see her come here."

"No, sir." The butler's expression did not alter. "Shall I bring her into the drawing room?"

"The library, I think."

The butler bowed again, and Edmund, coming into the large book-lined room, absently picked up a letter opener from his desk, tapping its blade against his palm, still frowning.

He wondered what crisis had prompted her to commit such an act of impropriety. He also remembered his mother's remark that her stepfather, Sir Matthew Prine, was far from a credit to his family, and she had shuddered as she had mentioned Tom Prine's imprisonment. She had not scrupled to mention Ellen Clive's unfortunate connection with her Hebraic music teacher—a mesalliance which had shocked society and resulted in the birth of a man who was actually receiving money for performing in public. Yet, as he had pointed out, none of these situations had any bearing on Tiffany's own impeccable background. The Clives were an old and blue-blooded family, and he had Lady Mary's sworn word that her first husband was a direct descendant of the Earls of Tyrconnel, one of Ireland's oldest families. This pedigree had proved soothing to his mother; and of course, there had been the favor of the Prince, which one could not discount, if one entertained political aspirations.

Of course, he also loved Tiffany. She was beautiful, charming, gracious, and would be an excellent wife and mother for the large family he meant to father—a baby every year was his ambition. He was fond of children and there was no better way to ensure the title remaining in the family. As an only son, he had always felt very nervous on that count. Consequently, the solecism she had committed in coming to his house must be overlooked. Of course, he would need to chide her a little, though nothing that would upset her too greatly. He would not want to do that, especially since she had been ill.

"Miss Prine," the butler said.

Edmund's smile of greeting faded as Tiffany entered. She was looking distressed but her blue eyes, usually so soft, were stormy, even defiant. "My dear," he said, coming to take her hand. To his surprise, she would not give it to him, going so far as to thrust it behind her back. Obviously she was in a strange humor. "My dear, what's amiss?" he asked concernedly.

To his consternation, she now held out her hand, palm upward. On it was her diamond engagement ring—a fine stone of the first water, which had belonged to his maternal grandmother, now put into a more modern setting. He regarded it perplexedly. "I do not understand."

"Edmund," she returned crisply, "I have come to relieve you from your obligations. I must tell you that marriage between us is impossible."

"My dear," he said in some distress, "will you not sit down?"

"No, I shall not stay long, though I fear I have already given rise to much speculation on the part of your servants, for which I am sorry. But there was no help for it."

"I beg you will not give it a thought, my love. I assure you that I do not."

A gleam of humor flickered in and out of her clear eyes. "And I am sure that you do, but no matter." She drew a deep breath. "I have done you a great wrong in agreeing to accept your proposal. I am not in love with you. I have never been in love with you; and while I am quite aware that love is not a prerequisite in a fashionable marriage, I am sure that I have led you to believe that I did cherish such feelings."

"My dear," he said soothingly, "I understand that you have been ill for the last week. I think you are still not yourself."

"Ill?" she repeated and then remembered her mother's words. The truth hovered on her tongue, but there was no need to complicate matters further. "Yes, I have been ill but that has naught to do with my change of mind. I shall not say change of heart, Edmund, because in that respect, my feelings have never changed. I have been in love with my Cousin Peter for most of my life and—"

"Love?" he interrupted sharply. "Infatuation, surely."

"Love," she replied steadily.

"But—" His lip curled. "My dear, you are young and impulsive and I cannot think you know your own mind. Until we went to his concert, you were certainly affectionate and warm to me and . . ."

She gave him a contrite glance. "I am very sorry for

154

that. I must tell you that I did try very hard to persuade myself that I loved you."

"And were most convincing," he said chokingly.

"I am sorry for that," she repeated.

"But, damn it!" he burst out. "You cannot do this to me! The wedding's been announced. I shall be a laughingstock. I shan't allow it. I am sure that your mother and father—"

"Stepfather," she corrected.

"Stepfather, then," he repeatedly angrily. "I am sure they'd not want you to bed a Jew."

She tensed, saying coldly, "You grow offensive, Edmund. Furthermore, you could as easily call him a British noble, for he is half a Clive, a Clive of Clive Abbey. However, I must tell you that his blood means nothing to me, who have felt his arms around me and his lips on mine."

His eyes were bright with fury. "How dare you tell me such immodest things?"

"Because they are true."

"If they be true, I shall send my seconds to him."

"I think you will not, Edmund."

"If he's dishonored you—"

"He has not dishonored me, even though I begged him to do so. I wanted him to take me to his bed; but however much you might despise his heritage, he was too honorable to accede to my request. Though I might add that he loves me as much as I love him. I might also tell you that I am desperately sorry that he did not bed me—I should have gloried in that dishonoring."

"You are shameless, wanton . . . no better than a Cyprian!" he thundered.

"I admit it freely. As far as Peter's concerned, I am all that you say and I am sure that you'd not wish to wed a Cyprian and so—here is your ring." She put it on the desk. "I bid you farewell."

His face was cold, expressionless. He said nothing as Tiffany went from the room. Once the door had closed on her, he picked up the ring and slipped it into his pocket. Out of a deep sense of outrage, he said loudly, "Shameless." Somehow the word helped to alleviate some part of the hollowness within his breast. "I have had a very narrow escape," he added. In less than two hours time, he had convinced himself that he believed it.

The stagecoach had started from the Black Swan Inn in London, and some four days later, it lumbered into its counterpart at York. Those passengers who had availed themselves of its facilities clambered from its unwieldly interior with relief. Despite the improved conditions on that highway known as the Great North Road, it had been a rough and, for some, a very disappointing journey—one they would not be eager to undertake soon again.

Two of them, a solicitor's clerk and a wealthy shopkeeper, were particularly put out because a third passenger, a slender, young woman, whose close-fitting bonnet and heavy veil did not prevent them from seeing that she was comely, had not provided the sport for which they had hoped. A woman traveling without even an abigail, might have been expected to provide rare sport, but when each of them, in turn, had tried to invade her room at the inns where they had spent the night, they had been confronted by a pistol, which though small, had looked extremely dangerous. Standing in the vicinity of the coach, they both visited angry glances upon her, to which she was quite impervious.

Tiffany, looking about her at the city's narrow, winding streets, many of which seemed absolutely medieval, was both hopeful and fearful. She had no assurance that Peter was at the abbey. All she knew was that his caretaker had been surprised at his precipitate departure, immediately he had returned from visiting his cousin. " 'E did not tell me where he was goin', miss," the man had said regretfully.

That he had gone had been a bitter disappointment at the time; but after some thought, she had made up her mind. Whether he were at the abbey or not, she would go to her Cousin Ellen. She, at least, would be glad to see her, and if Peter were gone to the continent, she would wait until he returned. She would wait forever. With that in mind, she had methodically set about making plans for her departure. She had sold her jewelry at a loss, but again, she did not care for that. She wanted only to leave London behind. She was glad she had purchased the pistol; it had stood her in good stead when those two ugly louts had tried to overpower her. Even though she had no more use for it, the little gun remained in her reticule. It was a long drive to the abbey, and one never knew what might happen on the roads.

As she went to hire the hackney that would take her to her journey's end, she wondered that she was not bone-weary, but she was not. She was buoyed up by an excitement she probably had no reason to feel, since it was very likely that Peter had gone to Vienna or even Rome. But perhaps he had not. By the time the hackney had passed through the abbey gates, she was sure he was not there and wondered why she had not asked the gatekeeper if he were in residence. As the vehicle started up the circular driveway, she signaled the coachman.

"Stop here, I shall walk the rest of the way."

She was trembling as she reached the door, and such was her state of mind, that by the time she had been ushered into the hall to confront an amazed Cousin Ellen, she was equally amazed to find herself inside. She could not remember knocking on the door or seeing it open. She had prepared a speech, explaining why she had come, explaining her mother's untoward actions. But all she could say was, "Is Peter come? I must see him. I . . ." She paused, hearing the faint, familiar sound of his violin.

Without another word, without heeding Cousin Ellen's words, she rushed down the hall to the music room and pulling the door open, came inside, slamming it shut behind her.

The music stopped mid-note.

His back was to her. It had stiffened. In a surprised and resentful tone, he said, "Mother, you—" and turning, stared at Tiffany incredulously. "You!"

His eyes were wide in his pale, drawn face—wide and, it seemed to her, filled with antagonism. She trembled, but she said staunchly, "I am very sorry to have interrupted your practicing, Peter. I know you do not like it. But I—I am here to remind you of your obligations." She paused, clutching her reticule and holding her breath.

"My obligations?" he repeated.

He was looking sad and somber and altogether unapproachable. She lifted her chin, looking him directly in the eye. "You promised faithfully to offer for me, and Mama tells me that you did not do so. Consequently, I have come to demand satisfaction." Reaching into her reticule, she drew out the little pistol. "You have trifled with my affections, sir, and shall pay the price unless you see fit to change your mind."

There was a moment when he stood absolutely still, when he said nothing. Then, his lips twitched, his eyes gleamed, and he broke into delighted laughter—delighted but tender, as well. Putting down his violin and bow, he strode to her and wrested the gun from her hand. Stopping only to place it by his violin, he threw his arms around her, kissing her even more passionately than he had a week earlier. When at length, he raised his head, he said softly, "Have I saved my life, my dearest love?"

"Oh, you *have,* Peter, you have—and mine, too."

YOUR WARNER LIBRARY OF REGENCY ROMANCE